Nevertheless, warm and fuzzy—among other sensations—just so happened to be exactly what Reed…or rather, Dr Atchison…aroused in her.

No, no, no, no, not *aroused*, she hastily corrected herself. No way did he *arouse* her. Never in a million years. She was a pregnant woman about to be tossed out of her home. The last thing she needed to be feeling these days was aroused by some guy she'd just met.

No, surely what Reed—Dr Atchison—did was, um…oh, gosh… Inspire her. Yeah, that was it. Pregnant women were always experiencing feelings of inspiration, weren't they? And hey, it was Christmas, after all. A very inspirational time of year. So it was *inspiration* she felt when faced with Reed Atchison. Inspiration, not arousal…

Dear Reader

Merry Christmas! We have six seasonal treats just for you in Desire this month.

Popular author Cait London gives us MAN OF THE MONTH, Tyrell Blaylock in *Typical Male*. He's another one of her Blaylock men; when they set their sights on something—or *someone*—there's no stopping them! Cait's back with another MAN OF THE MONTH in February 2001.

THE MILLIONAIRE'S CLUB concludes this month with Cindy Gerard's *Lone Star Prince*— where hero Greg Stone recognises the features of Princess Anna's four-year-old son as being remarkably like his own! We also begin a new trilogy by Elizabeth Bevarly, on a theme she's used before—FROM HERE TO MATERNITY. Look out for the next two titles in February and April 2001.

Maureen Child's back with another hunky Marine in *Marine Under the Mistletoe*. And there's a very special little person being delivered by Christmas in Christy Lockhart's *The Cowboy's Christmas Baby*. Finally, don't miss a classic fairy-tale-come-true in Kathryn Jensen's *I Married A Prince*.

Enjoy,

The Editors

A Doctor in Her Stocking

ELIZABETH BEVARLY

SILHOUETTE
DESIRE

*All the characters in this book have no existence outside the
imagination of the author, and have no relation whatsoever to anyone
bearing the same name or names. They are not even distantly inspired
by any individual known or unknown to the author, and all the
incidents are pure invention.*

*Silhouette, Silhouette Desire and Colophon
are registered trademarks of Harlequin Books S.A.,
used under licence.*

*First published in Great Britain 2000
Silhouette Books, Eton House, 18-24 Paradise Road,
Richmond, Surrey TW9 1SR*

© Elizabeth Bevarly 1999

ISBN 0 373 76252 6

22-1200

*Printed and bound in Spain
by Litografia Rosés S.A., Barcelona*

ELIZABETH BEVARLY

is an honours graduate of the University of Louisville and achieved her dream of writing full-time before she even turned thirty! At heart, she is also an avid traveller who once helped navigate a friend's thirty-five-foot sailboat across the Bermuda Triangle. 'I really love to travel,' says this self-avowed beach bum. 'To me, it's the best education a person can give to herself.' Her dream is to one day have her own sailboat, a beautifully renovated older-model forty-two footer, and to enjoy the freedom and tranquillity seafaring can bring. Elizabeth likes to think she has a lot in common with the characters she creates—people who know love and life go hand in hand. And she's getting some first-hand experience with motherhood, as well—she and her husband have a five-year-old son, Eli.

For Mum and Dad,
who always made Christmas wonderful.

One

"**T**errific. Nothing in today's paper, either."

In one hand, Mindy Harmon held the eviction notice with which her landlord had gifted her two weeks ago. In the other, she gripped the Monday real estate classifieds, wherein she could find not a thing to suit her needs—or, more correctly, her pocketbook. Again. And seeing as how Christmas was barely three weeks away, it wasn't likely that much would open up anytime soon. Certainly not within the thirteen days she had left before she would be forced out onto the street.

If she'd had a third hand, Mindy would have used it to comfort the new life growing in her womb. So, dropping the eviction notice onto her minuscule kitchen table—which, like the apartment and virtually everything else in it, was also rented—she curled her fingers over her softly budding torso, stroking with a slow, rhythmic caress.

"Looks like we're going to be homeless for Christmas, kiddo," she said softly, "unless some fairy godmother steps in to work some holiday magic for us."

She sighed heavily. Ah, well. This certainly wasn't the first setback she'd seen in her life, and, undoubtedly, it wouldn't be the last. Still, setbacks were a bit tougher to take now that she had someone besides herself to think about. Especially someone so tiny and defenseless, someone who would be relying solely on Mindy for his—or her—survival.

"Oh, Sam," she muttered aloud to her dead husband. "You really ruined Christmas this year, didn't you? And here I thought you'd never top the mess you made of things last year."

Of course, the catastrophe of last Christmas now paled in comparison to what the holiday promised to hold this year. Last year, all Sam Harmon had done was drink himself into oblivion and pass out on the Christmas tree. Of course, that, unfortunately, had resulted in the tree crashing into the fireplace. Which, even more unfortunately, had caused the tree to catch fire. And that, most unfortunately of all, had turned their entire house into a blazing tinderbox.

And as if all that *still* hadn't been enough to ruin the holiday, after the smoke had cleared, Sam, who had always, *always,* insisted on controlling the checkbook—because, hey, he was the man, and the man always took care of the finances, unless he was a total wuss—had revealed that he had neglected to pay a few bills here and there recently. Like, for example, their homeowner's insurance.

At least the two of them had come out of it alive. Homeless and penniless, but alive. And there had been a bright spot— the tragedy had made Sam finally realize that he needed to get help with his drinking. By summer, he'd been sober for nearly six months, and things had begun to look up. They'd even decided to start a family, and in August, Mindy learned she was expecting.

But the good times were short-lived. The day after she'd revealed her pregnancy to him, Sam started drinking again. And a few nights after that, on his way home from work via Stumpy's Bar and Grill, he'd driven into a tree at a much-higher-than-legal speed, and had been killed instantly.

Leaving Mindy, at twenty-seven years of age, widowed, expecting and broke. His life insurance had been just enough for her to bury him, pay off the mortgage for a house they didn't even have anymore and bail herself out of the massive credit card debt they'd accrued over the years, thanks to Sam's unrelenting spending. But there had been nothing—absolutely nothing—left to spare.

She supposed she should still be grieving for Sam—after all, it had only been four months since his death. But she'd had so many other things to think about in that time, so many other matters that had commanded her attention instead—taking care of herself and her unborn baby, making sure she had enough to eat and a place to sleep, and a way to pay for all the medical expenses, not to mention the endless array of things that the baby would need in the coming months. Sam hadn't given her much choice in the matter. He hadn't left her in a state where she could afford to grieve.

And, truth be told, their marriage had hardly been a happy one. They'd wed barely a month after meeting, and Mindy had realized—too late—that she really didn't know her husband at all. Instead of the handsome, charming, happy-go-lucky sort she had thought Sam to be, she'd quickly learned that he could be moody and unpredictable when he was drinking. And he drank a lot. Too much. Enough to put a significant strain on their marriage.

In spite of all that, though, she'd made up her mind early on that she *would* make the marriage a good one, no matter what she had to do. Marriage was for keeps, after all, till death—

Well, it was for keeps, that was all. And Mindy struggled for years to make hers work, to smooth over the rocky spots and stay the course. Sam, however, hadn't much shared her desire to keep things on track. More than once, he'd come home late smelling of bars and bourbon and beautiful women. Mindy had blamed his behavior on his drinking, but even in those all-too-few months of sobriety, even when the bars and bourbon were out of the picture, she knew the beautiful women weren't.

She had hoped becoming pregnant would make a difference for both of them. Sam had shared her enthusiasm for having a baby, had agreed wholeheartedly that he wanted to become a father as much as she wanted to be a mother. But, as always, he let her down there, too. Because the prospect of becoming a father—of having to be responsible for someone other than himself—had driven him right back to his old life-style.

Mindy sighed again as she tossed the classifieds down onto the table beside the eviction notice, splaying both hands open over her softly swollen belly. She was certainly no stranger to poverty, having grown up surrounded by it. And likewise, she was accustomed—pretty much—to being alone. Except for her four years married to Sam—which had been pretty lonely, too, now that she thought about it—she'd been alone since her mother's death when she was sixteen; she'd never known her father. And she was confident she could take care of herself, just as she had been doing for the last decade. But the little one… Ah, there was the worry. Because providing for herself was nothing compared to caring for a tiny, helpless life who would be solely dependent on her for survival.

She curled her fingers a little more possessively into her belly, battling the tears that threatened. Boy, pregnant women cried a lot, she thought. And she still had four months to go before the baby was born. Four months of complete uncertainty. Four months of wondering just how on earth she was going to manage to raise a baby on her meager income from waiting tables at a diner. Four months of feeling alone, frightened and anxious. Four months of worrying over how she was going to survive.

And then, once the baby was born, she knew, life would only hold more fear, more anxiety, more worry.

But, hey, that was four whole months away, she tried to reassure herself, swiping a quick finger under each eye. A lot could happen in four months. And she certainly wasn't as bad off as some people, she reminded herself. She had a roof over her head and a warm bed to sleep in—at least for another two weeks. And she had food in the refrigerator, heat in the radiator and a job that paid her a steady, if meager, wage.

And in three weeks, it would be Christmas, she recalled with a smile. This was the most wonderful time of the year. The most magical time of the year. The most hopeful time of the year.

Yeah, a lot could happen between now and the baby's birth. For the moment, at least, she…they…were okay. For the moment, she had everything she needed. For the moment, the balance of her life was just fine. She glanced down at her watch and frowned. And for the moment, she was running late for her shift, she realized. She was going to have to hustle if she wanted to make it to Evie's Diner in time for the after-work dinner rush.

Quickly, Mindy ran a brush through her unruly, shoulder length tresses, then bound them atop her head with a yellow ribbon, in a negligent heap of pale gold curls. A few pieces escaped to cascade around her face, but she didn't have time to fix them. Instead, she hastily donned her yellow waitress uniform and white tights, and stepped into her white sneakers. Then she thrust her arms through the sleeves of a white sweater to ward off the chill of a South Jersey winter while she was working, and grabbed her coat from the closet by the front door.

As she locked the door behind herself, she couldn't help but think that she would only be performing the gesture for another two weeks. Ed Franke—or, rather, Ed Cranky, as she inevitably thought of her joyless landlord—was throwing everyone out of the building, just in time to turn the place into a Christmas co-op. And with no family to turn to, there was nothing Mindy could do except find another place to stay once that due date arrived.

The phrase *due date* came back to haunt her as she raced down the stairs toward the street, stuffing her hands into her mittens as she went. Because even though the date of her eviction loomed far more heavily than the date of her baby's birth, frankly, Mindy wasn't ready for either of them. Unfortunately for her, though, there was no way she could avoid them. Because they would both be coming, all too soon.

Sure as Christmas.

Dr. Reed Atchison was in a lousy mood. But then, that wasn't really surprising, seeing as how, so far today, he'd overslept, nicked his chin something fierce while shaving, skidded off a snowy road into a pile of snow that couldn't have been more inconveniently placed and missed his turnoff on U.S. 31, thanks to unpredictable winter traffic—all of which had added up to making him late for work.

And that had just been that morning.

Since then, Reed had also had to intercede in a near-fracas between two dietary aides over whether Mr. Hunnicutt was on the bland or the high-fiber diet, and he'd had to tell Mrs. Wyatt Westaway that what she'd been certain was a life-threatening, malignant tumor in her chest was really only a gastric reaction spurred by her lactose intolerance. Plus, he had just come from four hours in surgery, and now he was hungrier than he'd ever been in his entire life. And as if all *that* weren't enough, to make matters even *worse,* on top of everything *else…*

He grumbled under his breath. On top of all that, it was Christmastime. *Christmastime.* Dammit. Just the thing to make a crummy day even crummier, and to make a scroogey man even scroogier.

Bah, humbug, he thought in the crummiest, scroogiest voice he could mentally muster. *What's for dinner?*

As if conjured by his thoughts, his colleague and what passed for his closest friend in the world, Dr. Seth Mahoney, strode into the locker room that all the male surgeons of Seton General Hospital shared. And as always, Seth was way too happy for Reed's tolerance. Way too warm. Way too sunny of disposition. Way too blond.

Honestly. How Reed and Seth had ever become friends in the first place was a complete and unsolvable mystery. They were opposites in every way, physical as well as metaphysical.

Reed's hair was black, his eyes brown, his features blunt and forbidding. He was the polar opposite of Seth's blond, blue-eyed, all-American-boyishness. Even their personal philosophies, and their outlooks on life, the universe and everything were totally at odds. Where Seth saw hope for the planet and the good in all people, Reed saw the truth—that they were all headed to hell in a handbasket. In the fast lane. Two at a time.

Total opposites, for sure. Seth, after all, *loved* this time of year.

"Reed!" the other man exclaimed when he saw Reed struggling to tug on his hiking boot. "Thank God you're here. I've just sewn Mr. Hoberman's scalp back on, and I'm ravenous for dinner. Care to join me?"

Reed chuckled in spite of himself. "Gee, Seth, put that way, I don't see how I can resist." He finished tying up his boots, then rose to jerk a massive, oatmeal-colored sweater on over his T-shirt and faded jeans. That done, he scrubbed both hands restlessly through his dark hair to tame it and rubbed his open palms over a day's growth of heavy beard.

"But it better be someplace casual," he added. "I'm not changing my clothes again. And I'm not in the mood to mind my manners, either."

"And this is news?" Seth pulled the top half of his pale blue hospital scrubs over his head, then dunked it easily into the laundry bin with a proud "Yesss!" for his perfect two-pointer. Which was no big deal, seeing as how the bin was only a foot away from the guy, Reed noted with a shake of his head. Then he went to work on his pants.

Once divested of his scrubs, he strode in his boxer shorts to the locker beside Reed's and wrestled it open. "I was thinking of trying that diner over on Haddonfield Road," he said, the metallic bang of the locker door punctuating his statement. "Evie's it's called. A couple of the nurses ate there the other night and raved about it."

"Fine," Reed said as he sat down to wait for his friend to finish dressing. "As long as there's food—and lots of it—it'll be perfect. I'm starving."

Seth's change of clothes was almost identical to Reed's, except that his own blue jeans were quite a bit more disreputable looking, and his sweater was a dark charcoal gray.

Jeez, he was blond, Reed thought as he eyed the other man critically. And so damn young to be such a skilled surgeon. Although Reed was only thirty-seven himself, he felt like he was decades older than Seth. Then again, Seth was the med school boy wonder who had graduated from high school at sixteen, completed his premed studies by nineteen and finished his residency three years ago, at the age of twenty-seven. So Seth hadn't exactly seen the same side of the world growing up that Reed had seen. And for that reason, he had doubtless aged a good bit more slowly.

To the casual observer, that observation would come as something of a surprise, because Reed Atchison was, and always had been, in a seemingly enviable position. He was a member of the generations-old, generations-rich Main Line Atchisons, one of the founding families of Philadelphia. His forebears had made their fortunes generations ago—one side of the family in steel, the other side in oil—and they'd hoarded every penny as if it would be the last they ever saw.

Reed still lived in the family stronghold in Ardmore, even though the massive house was way too big for a confirmed bachelor like himself. He kept a condo here in Cherry Hill, across the river and closer to the hospital, and he used it on those occasions when he didn't feel like making the drive home across Philadelphia.

He knew he should sell the estate now that both of his parents were gone. He was the last of the Atchisons and would almost certainly remain single and child-free, the end of the generational line. He had no desire to marry, certainly no desire to procreate and no desire to maintain all those family traditions that had been virtually engraved in stone—Italian marble, naturally—before he'd even been born.

Because for all their wealth and social prominence, the generations-old, generations-rich, Main Line Atchisons were also generations-cold and generations-closed-minded. Hell, Reed had had access to all the money and material possessions a kid could ever want when he was growing up. He'd attended all the best schools, had worn all the right clothes, had driven all the most bitchin' cars and had visited all the most happening vacation spots. But he sure could have used a hug or two along the way, and those had been glaringly absent from all the glitz and glamour.

The moment the thought materialized in his head, Reed shoved it away, frowning. Where the hell had that idea come from, anyway? He never had needed, never did need, never *would* need, a hug. Not now. Not ever. Hugs were... Well, they were... He fought off an involuntary shudder.

Unnecessary. That's what hugs were. Reed had lived for thirty-seven years just fine without excessive—or any, for that matter—physical shows of affection and he certainly wasn't going to start needing them now. Physical displays were way overrated, in his opinion. Signs of weakness.

Which was probably the main reason he'd partaken of so few of them in his life. Certainly he had a normal, healthy sex drive but he'd had little impulse to act on it over the years. He told himself it was because he just didn't meet that many women he wanted to be physical with. And, hey, in this day and age, sex could get you killed. No, he didn't exactly live like a monk. But he wasn't a party animal, either. Most of his relationships had ended when the women lost interest, usually because he didn't show them the kind of physical attention they demanded.

These days, Reed lived a quiet, uneventful, orderly life and he liked it that way just fine. Why mess it all up with a relationship, especially one that would include...hugging?

It was just that this time of year was so full of that stuff, he thought, conveniently blaming the holiday he'd always resented for his emotional restlessness of late. Everywhere he looked, people were getting maudlin and sentimental. All the magazines were sporting covers that depicted more-illuminated-than-usual family life. All the television commercials showed sappy scenes of homecoming and reunion, over and over and *over* again. Everyone everywhere was wishing him a happy holiday, every time he turned around.

Like Reed would ever have a happy holiday. Or a homecoming or reunion. Or even a more-illuminated-than-usual family life. No sense in getting all maudlin and sentimental. It could only lead to trouble.

"Hey, man, you look like you could use a hug."

Reed jerked up his head to glower at his friend's assessment, only to find Seth holding back his laughter.

"I do not want to go there," Reed muttered as he stood, suddenly oddly delighted by the fact that he was a good three inches taller and twenty pounds heavier than his friend. All of it solid rock, naturally, he thought further.

"Then quit looking like you just lost your best friend," Seth told him, still smiling.

"Don't tempt me," Reed returned, only half joking.

But Seth wasn't falling for it. "C'mon, Reed, it's Christmas. Will you please just lighten up?"

"Christmas," Reed echoed blandly. "All the more reason to feel cranky." Then, just for good measure, he added, "Bah, humbug."

"Oh, thank you so much, Dr. Scrooge, for that enlightening, yet seasonal, observation." Seth shook his head in what was clearly feigned disgust. "You know, I'm really glad I didn't spring for the Russell Stovers for you this year. You'll have to make do with an old, fossilized Hershey bar I found under my sofa cushion last July."

"Just don't wrap it, okay?" Reed said. "I hate all that festive red and green."

But Seth only chuckled some more. "I have never met a man more predisposed to holiday grumpiness than you are. I'm sure there must be a reason for it, and if you were really my friend, you'd tell me what it was, but..." With what sounded like a heartfelt sigh, he shut his locker door with a resounding *clank* and turned to Reed. "I guess, for now, I'll just have to look for the best in you."

This time Reed was the one to chuckle, but his dry, derisive laughter in no way mirrored the good humor his friend's had held. "If you want to find the best in me, then you'll have to dig pretty damned deep," he said.

"Hey, no problem," Seth answered readily. "I'm a surgeon, remember? A really good one, too. I know what's deep inside everyone. And I have a college degree to prove it."

He knew what was deep inside everyone, huh? Reed mused. Now there was a troubling thought.

But before he could comment, Seth continued. "See, that's where we differ," he said.

"Only there?"

Reed's sarcasm went right over his friend's head. Either that or, like always, Seth just chose to ignore it. Because he went on, "When I go into a person, I'm looking for the good stuff and I work with that. And when *you* go in, you're looking for the bad, and that takes priority."

"Is this some weird surgeon's angle on the glass being half-full or half-empty?"

Seth nodded. "Yeah, in a way, I guess it is. I'm just saying that I refuse to be blinded by the bad things in life, when those are so few and far between. It's the good things that are most obvious, most evident, most abundant. And those are what make us able to survive the bad things."

"Oh, please. You can't possibly believe that the good in the world outweighs the bad. There's poverty, hatred, bigotry, terrorism, war—"

"Love, honor, education, beauty, art," Seth immediately interrupted him.

But Reed wasn't going to let him get away that easily. "Sickness, death, crime, drugs," he continued to enumerate.

Seth, however, was no more willing to back down than Reed was. "Music, chocolate, lingerie, prime rib—"

"All right, all right," Reed surrendered. "Let's just agree to disagree, okay?"

But Seth shook his head. "No, I don't agree to do that."

Reed eyed him in confusion. "You always did before."

"It's Christmas," he repeated unnecessarily. "This is the

best time of year to focus on the good things. Frankly, I'm getting really tired of all your pessimism.''

Reed opened his mouth to object, but Seth held up a hand, palm out, to cut him off. ''Just hear me out,'' he said. ''I'm going to make a little wager with you, to prove that I'm right and you're wrong.''

Now Reed eyed his friend with suspicion. ''What are you talking about?''

Seth settled his hands on his hips, staring at his friend with much consideration. ''You insist that the bad outweighs the good in people, right?''

Reed nodded. ''Didn't I make that obvious?''

Seth ignored his question and asked instead, ''You are of the opinion that man is, by nature, at best, indifferent, right?''

Another nod. ''Right.''

''You think the average person is more likely to turn his back on someone in need than to lend that person a helping hand, correct?''

''Correct.''

Seth paused, then crossed his arms over his chest and eyed Reed some more. ''I, on the other hand, am convinced that the good outweighs the bad, that people are, by nature, decent folk and that, if given a choice, the average person will be inclined to help out another individual in need.''

''My, what a rebel you are,'' Reed responded dryly. ''Hang on a second while I alert the media.''

But Seth only ignored him again. ''And I'm going to bet you that *I'm* right and *you're* wrong.''

Reed smiled. He loved betting with Seth. Because, invariably, Seth lost. He was a lousy gambler, doubtless because he was such a flagrant optimist. Optimists never came out ahead in wagers. There was no place for hope in the world of chance. But instead of leaping to agree to the other man's offer, Reed hesitated.

''What's in it for me, if I win?'' he asked. ''More important, what's in it for you, if I lose? And just how the hell are we supposed to settle something like this anyway? It's all abstract.''

"It's Christmas," Seth repeated, more emphatically this time. "That means goodwill toward humankind abounds out there right now. You sure you want to go through with this wager? Things are heavily weighed in my favor."

"Oh, please," Reed muttered. "Christmas makes no difference at all. People still hate each other, they're still willing to take advantage of each other. Now more than ever, I'd bet. There must be no end to the holiday scams that arise this time of year."

"I say you're wrong," Seth insisted. "I predict that within hours of our walking out of this hospital, we'll witness some act of goodwill that was totally unprovoked."

Reed narrowed his eyes at his friend. "What do you mean?"

"I mean that you and I—" he punctuated the statement by pointing a finger first at Reed, then at himself "—we're going to spend the rest of the evening together. And before this evening is through, I'll bet you that we see someone do something nice for someone else. For no other reason than that it was the right and decent thing to do, because one person cared about what happened to another."

Reed glanced down at his watch. "There's less than five hours left to this evening, pal," he said. "Don't you think you're being a little optimistic?"

Seth smiled. "Uh, yeah. That was kind of the point, Reed. It just goes to show you how absolutely certain I am that I'll win."

"You're out of your mind," Reed assured him. "But I don't have any problem taking advantage of a crazy man. As long as the prize is right. What do I win at the end of this evening, when you realize what a sap you've set yourself up to be?"

Now Seth's smile turned predatory. "If you win—which, it goes without saying, you won't—I'll spring for an all-expenses-paid golf holiday in Scotland next summer. For two. You and me. Won't cost you a dime.''

Reed thought about that for a minute. "Throw in a bottle of The MacCallan, and you're on.''

"You got it,'' Seth agreed readily. "But if I win,'' he hastily continued, before Reed had a chance to start feeling cocky, "then I get something of equal value in return.''

"You want me to pay for a trip to Scotland for two? I can do—''

"No,'' Seth told him. "What I want in return is for Dr. Scrooge to perform an act of humanity, of goodwill, himself. A gesture of complete selflessness and kindness.''

"*What?*'' Reed exclaimed.

"If I win,'' Seth said, "then you have to do something nice for somebody.''

Reed threw his friend a look that he knew must be ripe with suspicion. Because suspicious was exactly how he was feeling at the moment. "I have to do something nice for someone? That's all?''

Seth barked out a laugh this time. "*That's all?*'' he echoed incredulously. "Listen to you. You act like it won't cost you anything to perform an act of selfless kindness for someone.''

Reed's suspicion compounded at the statement. "It won't,'' he told the other man.

Seth smiled, a smile that was knowing, confident and a bit sad. "Then how come you've never done something nice for anyone before?'' he asked softly.

Reed opened his mouth to reply but realized, much to his dismay, that he had no idea what to say. He *hadn't* ever done anything nice for anyone before, he thought. Had he? He tried to remember. But he honestly couldn't come up with a single incident where he had committed an act of selfless, unprovoked, unpremeditated…niceness.

It wasn't that he had anything against gestures of goodwill, he tried to assure himself. He just didn't trust them. And he wasn't a bad man. He was just a…a thoughtless man? An uncaring man? No, surely not, he told himself. He was

thoughtful. He was caring. He thought and cared about…stuff.
Sure, he did. It had just never occurred to him to…what was
it that bumper sticker said? Commit Acts of Random Kindness
and Senseless Beauty? But the reason for that was simply because he wasn't one much for bumper-sticker philosophy, that
was all.

Wasn't it?

"I…" he began. But no more words were forthcoming.

"You what?" Seth cajoled.

"I…" Reed tried again.

"What?"

"I…I accept your wager," he finally finished lamely. "If I
lose—which I won't," he hastened to add, "I'll even throw
in a bottle of The MacCallan."

Seth nodded, and Reed got the feeling the other man knew
something he didn't know himself. But all he said was,
"Good. Then let's eat."

TWO

Mindy had never been more exhausted in her entire life than she was as the dinner rush began to wind down. Boy, the first trimester had been bad enough, she thought, had had her nodding off at the worst times, in the strangest places. She'd once fallen asleep while riding the elevator to the OB-GYN's office. She recalled reading somewhere that women were supposed to have a burst of energy in the second trimester. They were supposed to feel strong and animated and invincible, like some kind of prenatal Wonder Woman.

Mindy, however, felt more like Washer Woman.

"Order up, Mindy!"

She sighed heavily, hoisting herself up from the chair behind the counter where she'd collapsed in the hopes of stealing a minute or two off her feet. Then, when a rush of wintry wind blasted her from the door that was opening ahead of two more diners, she hugged her sweater more tightly around herself. She was almost as cold these days as she was tired. She hadn't felt warm for five months now.

She stood up on tiptoe to pluck the Reuben sandwich and fries from the kitchen window, settling them onto her tray before reaching up to retrieve their mate, a chicken salad on whole wheat. And as she crossed the diner to present both plates to their rightful owners, another patron lifted a hand, indicating he wanted to place an order. Mindy nodded as she took care of one table before approaching the other, tugging a stubby pencil from beneath her by-now-dismembered pony-tail as she made her way to the newcomer.

She smiled as she stopped by his table, so much did he resemble Santa Claus—a really skinny Santa Claus, anyway. But where Santa's dapper red suit looked plenty warm, this guy's attire was neither red nor dapper, nor did it look in any way warm. His tweed jacket was threadbare, his gloves more hole than wool. A knit cap covered his ears, but she couldn't believe the man received much warmth from it.

Poor thing, she thought. It must be in the twenties out there tonight—so far, December had been unseasonably cold—and he probably didn't have anyplace else to go. She thanked her lucky stars again that she wasn't out on the streets—yet—and conjured the most winning smile from her arsenal.

"What can I get for you?" she asked the man.

He smiled back at her, and although he may have been cold on the outside, he certainly radiated warmth from within. "I'm celebratin'," he said without preamble.

Mindy chuckled, so infectious were his high spirits. "Good for you," she told him. "What's the occasion?"

"It's my birthday," he replied proudly, his voice sounding rusty from disuse but happy nonetheless.

"Hey, congratulations. Is it the big three-oh?" she teased, because, clearly, it had been decades since this man had seen thirty.

He laughed and shook his head. "I'm eighty years old to-day, missy. *Eighty!* What d'ya think about that?"

"Get out!" she exclaimed, nudging his bony shoulder play-fully with her elbow. "And here I thought I was going to have to card you if you asked for a beer."

He laughed some more. "No, ma'am. I don't touch that stuff. But I think I might like to sample some of that chili I hear they do so good here."

Mindy nodded as she scribbled down his order. "It's the best," she assured him. "Evie's special recipe, passed down through generations. What else can I get for you?"

The man's smile dimmed some. "Maybe just a glassa water. That oughta do me."

She started to object, started to remind him that it was his birthday and that he was entitled to celebrate with more than just a bowl of chili, then she realized that a bowl of chili was probably all he could afford to buy. And heaven only knew how long he'd been saving to manage even that for a birthday feast.

So she smiled once more, tucking her pencil back into her hair, and said, "I'll be right back with your water."

Among other things, she thought. She rattled the change in her pocket as she strode toward the carousel over the kitchen window. She'd had a good night tonight, considering the fact that it was Monday. Thanks to the nearby mall and hospital, Evie's Diner always had a nice, steady stream of patrons, both from people who worked in those places and the people visiting them. Heck, Mindy had probably cleared almost twenty bucks this shift, in addition to her—very tiny, granted—wages. Still, there was no reason she couldn't spring for a little birthday present for someone who was marking such a major milestone.

She made a few more notations to the man's order, then clipped it onto the carousel and spun it around to the kitchen. "Order in, Tom!" she called to the cook. Then she went to the coffeepot to fill a cup of hot birthday cheer for her customer.

"The club sandwich looks good."

Reed mumbled something in agreement to Seth's gourmet analysis, but his attention wasn't on the plastic-coated menu in his hand. It was on the blond, pale, exhausted-looking—

and slightly pregnant—waitress on the other side of the diner, the one who seemed to be *this* close to falling over if one more stiff wind from outside hit her. Involuntarily, his gaze skidded over to the main entrance as two more diners strode through. He had to force himself not to shout, "Hey! Close the damned door, will ya?" or jump up to close it himself.

Fortunately, when he looked over at her again, he saw that the little blond waitress had moved behind the counter to sit down. Reed mentally willed the newcomers to take a seat in somebody else's section and glanced down at the menu again.

Hmm… The club sandwich *did* look pretty good. Of course, at this point, he was so hungry that a rubber chicken with a wax apple stuck in its mouth would look good.

"No, the French dip, I think," Seth was saying.

But again, Reed's attention had been diverted, because wouldn't you know it, those two idiots who had just come in had indeed sat down at one of the exhausted-looking waitress's tables, and she was making her way toward them now.

He felt he could honestly say that he'd never met a weak woman in his entire life. Never. The doctors and nurses of the feminine persuasion who surrounded him at the hospital were in no way fragile, in no way weak. On the contrary, they were the hardiest, sturdiest people he knew, both physically and emotionally. And the women in his family, both Atchisons on his father's side and Thurmons on his mother's side, had been uncommonly stalwart. Strong-willed, strong-minded, strong-tempered.

Which maybe explained why he couldn't take his eyes off of the waitress who seemed to be none of those things. She was an alien creature of sorts, a fragile female. And something inside Reed—something he had never felt before in his entire life—surged up out of nowhere, nearly overwhelming him. A desire to protect her, he marveled. To take care of her. That was what the something welling up inside him was. She was a total stranger, he tried to remind himself. And probably not quite as fragile as she appeared.

Still…

He shook off the incomplete rumination as he watched her. In spite of her obvious exhaustion and her faintly rounded belly, she moved with certainty and purpose. And even though she looked ready to collapse, she stood firm—even smiled a little—as she scribbled down an order on her pad and moved away from the table. She joked with the elderly man seated in the booth across from Reed and Seth, and her laughter sounded robust enough as it warmed the room around her.

And still Reed couldn't quite take his eyes off of her. Still, he felt compelled to do something—he had no idea exactly what—to ease her fatigue.

He told himself it was because she was pretty, in a pale, fragile kind of way, and any man worth his weight in testosterone would just naturally respond to that. But there must be something else, too, he mused. Because he'd been around women who were prettier than she was, women who wore much-more-attractive outfits than a yellow polyester waitress uniform and sneakers. And they hadn't come close to capturing his attention the way this woman had.

She *was* pretty, though. And she smiled a lot. And even though she seemed fragile, there was something about her that indicated she probably could take care of herself just fine. That maybe she *had* been taking care of herself for some time now. He supposed looks could be deceiving. And after all was said and done, she really was none of his business.

Still, he thought, she *was* pretty.

"Definitely the French dip," Seth said, bringing Reed's thoughts back to the matter at hand—food.

Their waitress—a brash, blousy brunette whose name tag proclaimed her to be Donna—returned then, and Seth repeated his order for her. Reed asked for the club sandwich because he'd never read past it—and, hey, it did look good—along with coffee. He was about to ask for a side of onion rings when a quiet outburst of laughter erupted from the other side of the room, claiming not only his attention but Seth's and their waitress's as well.

"'Scuse me for a minute, will you, gents?" she asked as

she moved away from their table and over to the one across the way.

As Reed and Seth watched, every waitress in the place, along with the cashier, the busboy and a couple of gravy-stained kitchen workers, gathered around the other booth and began belting out a rousing rendition of "Happy Birthday" to the elderly man seated there. He seemed not to know what to make of the episode at first, then he smiled, a huge grin that softened his craggy features and actually brought tears to his eyes.

Tears, Reed marveled. Just because a bunch of diner employees were singing "Happy Birthday" to him. Unbelievable. He shook his head in bemusement, then turned to say something to Seth. But he stopped short, because, naturally, Seth was looking as if he wanted to burst into tears himself.

Oh, man. What a pushover.

"Why don't you just go over and join them for another chorus?" Reed asked, only half joking.

But Seth didn't rise to the bait. "Hey, if they sing another chorus, maybe I will."

"You are such a bleeding heart."

"Hey, at least I have a heart to bleed."

Meaning, of course, that Reed didn't have a heart, he thought grimly. Then again, he couldn't exactly deny Seth's assertion, could he? Not when he went out of his way, every single day of his life, to illustrate exactly that fact. Hey, it was hereditary, after all. Heartlessness ran on both sides of his family tree.

"Why is it that you became a neurologist?" Reed suddenly asked the other man. "You'd do much better with hearts."

"Ironic, isn't it?" Seth returned dryly. "You being a cardiologist, I mean, seeing as how *you* would do so much better with heads."

"Maybe I just like cutting them open," Reed said, unable to help himself. "Or better yet, cutting them out."

"Or maybe," Seth posed, "you're just trying to figure out

what makes them tick. Trying to learn how to jump-start your own."

Reed eyed him thoughtfully, thinking he should probably be offended by what Seth had said. Oddly, he wasn't. In spite of that, he responded, "You know, that's a hell of a thing for a man to say to his best friend."

"Yeah, it is, isn't it?" Seth agreed. "Makes you think, doesn't it?"

"What's that supposed to mean?"

Seth was spared having to answer that question by the return of their waitress, who was still chuckling when she pulled her pencil from behind her ear again. With a couple of quick cracks of her gum, she sighed out a final laugh and said, "Oh, that was fun. Now then. Can I get anything else for youse? Coffee? Beer?"

Reed was about to ask for those onion rings again, but Seth gestured toward the other table and piped up, "What was that all about?"

Donna smiled, one of those too-bright, why-don't-you-come-up-to-my-place-and-see-my-etchings? kind of smiles. And Seth, naturally, returned it with one of his own. Seth always had liked brash, blousy brunettes. And brash, blousy blondes. Brash, blousy redheads, too. And really, they didn't have to be brash. Or blousy, either, for that matter. As long as they were breathing.

"That," Donna said, "was yet another one of Mindy's good deeds. The kid's got a heart of gold. Go figure."

Well, that certainly perked Seth right up, Reed noticed. Not that Seth needed perking. He was just about the perkiest damned man on the planet already.

"Good deed?" he echoed. "Heart of gold? Gosh, that's really, really interesting. And just who, may I ask, is Mindy?"

Donna jutted her stubby pencil over her shoulder, toward the pretty—pregnant—blond waitress who had commanded so much of Reed's attention. "She's a total sweetheart, that's who Mindy is," she told them. "Like I said, go figure. In the last year, her house burned to the ground, her husband got himself killed and every nickel she had left went to straightening out the mess he'd made of their lives. And now she's being evicted from her crummy apartment so the scumbag landlord can turn it into a co-op. *And* she's five months preggers, to boot. *And* broke. *And* all she has is this lousy-paying job to get her through. But even at that, she bought the old guy dinner tonight, because it's his eightieth birthday.''

"Oh, *really?*" Seth asked with *much* interest, folding an elbow onto the table and cupping his chin in his palm. "My, but that was *certainly* a nice thing for her to do."

Reed frowned, knowing where this was going. "So that must be her grandfather or something, right?" he asked, jerking his head toward the elderly man across the way.

Donna shook her head, her dark ponytail dancing when she did. "Naw, she never saw the guy before tonight. He's homeless, I think. Prob'ly usually gets his dinner out of the Dumpster out back."

"Oh, *really?*" Seth reiterated. "She'd never met him before tonight? He was a total stranger to her?"

"Yeah, but on account of it's his birthday, he came in and ordered a bowl of chili, 'cause he wanted to celebrate. But Mindy thought he should get more than just a bowl of chili, so she used some of her tips to buy him a cuppa coffee and a steak sandwich and a piece a peach pie to go with."

"Oh, *really?*"

Donna, finally, gave him a funny look. "Yeah, *really.* Boy, it doesn't take much to interest you, does it?"

Seth threw her a salacious grin and cocked one blond eyebrow. "You might be surprised."

Donna tossed him a pretty lascivious smile right back. "Oh, yeah?"

Reed cleared his throat in a manner that was by no means discreet. "Uh, do you think you could go ahead and place that order now?" he asked. He was, after all, going to take a bite out of the table if someone didn't put something edible in front of him soon.

"Yeah, sure thing," Donna said, turning.

Reed was about to add that extra part about onion rings before she could get away, but before he had a chance Seth caught her gently by the elbow and said, "So this Mindy has nothing in the world, is about to be bounced out of her apartment, along with her unborn child, but she squeezed out a few bucks from her tips just so this old guy she'd never met before could have a decent birthday dinner?"

Donna scrunched up her shoulders and let them drop. "Didn't I just say that?"

Reed nodded and released her. "Yeah, you did. But I wanted to make sure my friend here heard all the details."

"I heard," Reed muttered.

As always, Seth ignored him. "Thanks, Donna," he said instead, releasing their waitress so that she could place their order. Finally.

"No problem, big guy," she returned with a bright smile. "I'll be right back with your coffee."

And then she was gone. Before Reed could tell her how much he wanted those onion rings. He sighed with much disappointment.

"Did you hear that, Reed?" Seth asked, turning to sit forward at the table again.

"I heard," Reed repeated.

"Mindy, that big, selfless, generous sweetheart, did that out of the *goodness* of her heart."

"I heard."

"Just because it was the *right thing to do*."

"I *heard*."

"Because she's a *kind, decent human being*."

"I *heard*, dammit."

Seth leaned back in his seat, crossing his arms with *much* satisfaction, grinning triumphantly. "Can you imagine?"

Reed ground his teeth hard. "According to our waitress, she's also pregnant," he pointed out. "It was probably just some kind of maternal instinct or hormonal reaction kicking in."

Seth chuckled. "Yeah, you wish."

There was no way Reed was going to get out of this one, he thought. Seth had gotten lucky tonight. He'd taken a chance that they'd encounter some bleeding heart like himself, and for once in his life, the guy's gamble had played out. Which meant no golfing vacation in Scotland. No bottle of thirty-six-year-old, single-malt scotch. But worse than all that, now Reed was going to have to do something…nice…for somebody.

In a word, *ew*.

"All right, you win," he conceded. "I'll perform a good deed. Can I just write a check to the Salvation Army?"

Seth smiled. "Of course you can. But don't think for a moment that doing so will settle our wager."

"I was afraid you'd say that."

"You have to perform a good *deed*," his friend reminded him. "A physical act of niceness and goodwill. Check writing is too impersonal. But by all means, you can include a check to some deserving organization as part of your payment for your debt."

"Fine."

"But you know who could probably really use a helping hand right about now?" Seth added.

Reed narrowed his eyes. He could tell by the other man's tone of voice that he wasn't going to like the suggestion that would inevitably follow.

"Mindy, that's who."

Yep, Reed had known he wasn't going to like his friend's suggestion at all.

"I mean, think about it," Seth continued. "She's pregnant, she's about to be evicted. And just three weeks before Christmas, too. *Evicted,* do you believe that? What kind of scumbag landlord does such a thing?"

Reed frowned at him. "Uh, yeah, I do believe that, Seth. I'm the one who expects the worst from everybody, remember?"

Seth gave that some thought. "Oh, yeah. Well, there you have it. Sometimes you're right. Not usually," he quickly interjected when Reed opened his mouth to pounce on the concession. "But sometimes. Anyway, getting back to Mindy…"

"I'd rather not."

"I think she'd be a likely recipient for your goodwill," Seth went on, ignoring, as always, Reed's objection.

"Fine. Then I'll write *her* a check."

Seth shook his head. Vehemently. "No, no, no, no, *no*. You're missing the whole point. You have to *do* something nice for her. A good *deed*."

"Hey, writing a check is doing something. It involves a physical activity."

Seth made a face at him. "You know what I mean." Then, before Reed could utter another word, his friend lifted a hand and called out, "Oh, Mindy! Excuse me, Mindy?"

Reed squeezed his eyes shut tight. He could not believe what was happening. He felt as if he was in seventh grade again and his best buddy, Bobby Weatherly, was about to reveal the crush Reed had had on Susan Middleton. Man, that had been humiliating. To this day, Reed simply could not speak to any woman named Susan without feeling embarrassed. Now it looked as if he was going to have the same problem with all future Mindys.

The little blond waitress appeared to be understandably confused as she approached their table but she didn't seem at all anxious. As she drew nearer, though, Reed saw that she looked even more fragile and exhausted than she had from a distance. Her eyes were smudged by faint purple crescents, her cheeks were overly pink, as if she'd exerted herself far too much this evening. Her face had a thin, pinched look to it, as if her pregnancy so far had left her drained.

As a doctor, even if he was a cardiologist instead of an obstetrician, he knew pregnancy hit different women different ways. Some women continued on with their lives as if there were nothing out of the ordinary going on with their bodies. Some women had more energy than ever. And some, like Mindy, were left looking almost ghostlike, thanks to the extra work their bodies were forced to perform in order to generate life.

She wrapped her sweater more tightly around herself as she paused by their table. Her gaze lit first on Seth, and then on Reed, then quickly ricocheted back to Seth, as if she'd been troubled by something in Reed's expression.

"Can I help you?" she asked.

Her voice, too, was thin and fragile, soft, but warm. She looked to be in her midtwenties, Reed thought, even if she did carry herself like an old woman. The other waitress's words came back to him, almost as if he hadn't heard them clearly the first time. She said Mindy's husband had "gotten himself killed," thereby leaving this young woman a widow. She'd suffered a very significant—and very recent, seeing as how her pregnancy was barely showing—tragedy, and now she was about to suffer another in being evicted from her home.

Why did life do that to some people? he wondered. Why did it just keep hitting them and hitting them and hitting them, then kicking them again for good measure when they were down? Why were some people singled out from others to receive the lion's share of misfortune? It wasn't fair. It wasn't right. People like this pale, fragile woman surely deserved better than that.

"My friend and I couldn't help but overhear that rousing rendition of 'Happy Birthday,'" Seth said, scattering Reed's thoughts. "Nor could we help but notice that you seemed to be leading the choir."

Mindy smiled. "Yeah, it was great, wasn't it? Well, not the singing necessarily," she quickly qualified with an even brighter smile. "I know I have a long way to go before I could be a Supreme. I meant it's great that Mr. McCoy has reached his eightieth birthday. Eighty! Isn't that amazing?" she asked, her voice growing more animated. "I mean, think about it. He's lived through the Roaring Twenties, the Depression, World War II, the Race for Space, the Cold War, Vietnam…"

"And he survived leisure suits and the disco era, too," Seth added. "No mean feat, that."

Mindy nodded. "Exactly. The world has changed so much in his lifetime. And he can remember all of it. It's incredible."

Reed looked over at Seth and found his friend hanging on Mindy's every word, as if she were revealing the secrets of the universe to him. "Incredible," he echoed in a voice that Reed had heard before, the one Seth used when he was fast falling for a woman he shouldn't be falling for, fast or otherwise.

Of course, Seth fell fast for a new woman nearly every hour, which meant that Reed should put a stop to his descent right now. That way he could spare the innocent Mindy the ugly aftermath of his friend's wandering ways.

"Miss, uh…" Reed began.

The waitress turned to him, but where she'd had a sunny smile in place for Seth, her features quickly schooled into a polite, if bland, expression for him. "Mindy is fine," she told him.

Yes, Mindy is indeed fine, Reed thought before he could stop himself.

That thought was immediately followed by another, one that essentially went, *Holy cow! Where did that come from?* Immediately, he pushed both thoughts away. She was pregnant, for God's sake, he reminded himself. No way did she deserve to be ogled like a…like a…like a beautiful woman, he finished lamely. Even if that was precisely what she was. She was a beautiful woman. One who was waif thin and delicate looking.

She was in no way the kind of woman he normally ogled, anyway, pregnant or otherwise. He preferred women his own age, professional women in his own income bracket, women who'd shared some of the same life experiences he'd had himself. Strong women. Women who didn't look so damned exhausted and…well, fragile.

"Mindy," he said. "You'll have to excuse my friend here. He's easily impressed."

She nodded, but somehow he knew she had no idea what he was talking about. "Well, enjoy your dinner," she said hastily, turning away.

"Wait," Seth exclaimed, halting her progress, "don't go."

She spun around again, but this time her expression was unmistakably wary. "Was there something else? I'll be happy to go get Donna for you."

"No, no," Seth told her. "It's what *we* can do for *you*. Or rather, what my friend and colleague can do for you. Because, Mindy, sweetheart, Dr. Atchison here is about to make you an offer you can't refuse." Seth turned his attention pointedly on Reed and asked, "Aren't you, old buddy, old pal?"

Mindy eyed first the blond man in the booth before her, and then the black-haired one…and felt the hairs on the back of her neck leap to attention. The two men were like color negatives of each other: one handsome, fair and blue-eyed, the other handsome, dark and brown-eyed. Their dispositions, too, seemed to be utterly opposite each other. Where the blonde put Mindy immediately at ease and seemed pleasant enough, the dark-haired man sent every sense on alert and made her entire body hum with electricity.

Not that he seemed scary by any stretch of the imagination. Not in a dangerous way, at any rate. He did, however, inspire a kind of caution, the kind a woman felt when faced with a man who had the potential to break her heart. Strange, that, she thought, seeing as how she'd only known him for about thirty seconds now.

Although both men were certainly attractive, the blonde was a bit too boyish in his looks, a bit too adorable in his presentation, for Mindy to find him anything other than kind of cute. The dark-haired man, however…

Well, she'd always been partial to black hair. And brown eyes. And craggy, blunt good looks. Which made her choice of husband odd, now that she thought more about it, because Sam Harmon had been a sandy-haired, blue-eyed, surfer-dude wannabe. Therefore, this man was nothing at all like Sam. And therefore, she told herself, she shouldn't feel intimidated by him the way she had felt around Sam there toward the end.

And really, intimidated was the last thing she felt at the

moment. As standoffish as the dark-haired man's demeanor seemed to be, Mindy immediately sensed something within him—way deep down within him—that was almost... personable? Warm? Good-hearted? Kind? Oh, no, surely not, she corrected herself. Not with a frown like that. Not with a glare like that.

Still...

"He really is going to make you an offer you can't refuse," the blond man said, shaking off the odd sensation winding its way through Mindy's soul. "Just watch. Reed?" he said further. "Tell our studio audience what Mindy here has won."

She eyed the dark-haired man—the one called Reed—in confusion, then turned back to the blonde. "I'm sorry," she said. "But you guys seem to have me at a loss. I have no idea what you're talking about."

She waited for the blond man to offer an explanation—or even the dark man, for that matter. She wasn't particular, so long as she received *some* kind of explanation—and when none was forthcoming, she arched her eyebrows in silent query.

Finally taking the hint, the blond man dipped his head toward his companion. "My friend here," he said, "is Dr. Reed Atchison, resident heart surgeon over at Seton General Hospital. I," he added hastily, seeming genuinely surprised to realize that he had neglected to introduce himself as well, "am Dr. Seth Mahoney. And Reed and I have been having an interesting difference of opinion lately. You, my dear Miss...uh, Mindy...have just solved the dilemma for us."

Mindy eyed him warily. "Um, thanks. I guess."

"No, no, thank *you*," he immediately—and very enthusiastically—replied. "This has been a most enlightening meal, and we haven't even received our food yet."

"We haven't received our coffee yet, either," the dark-haired man—Reed...Dr. Atchison—mumbled.

"Oh, I'll go get Donna and remind her," Mindy offered quickly, snatching the opportunity to excuse herself from what was promising to become a puzzling—if not outright bizarre—situation.

"Not yet," the blonde—Seth...Dr. Mahoney...whoever—halted her.

She sighed fitfully. "I'm really sorry," she said again, "but I don't know what you guys are talking about, and I have a lot of work to do right now, so if you'll just excuse me..."

The blond M.D. nodded. "I understand," he said. Gosh, that made one of them, Mindy thought dryly. Before she could comment, however, he added, "We can continue our conversation after your shift has ended."

Mindy shook her head. "Oh, I don't think that would be—"

"It's no problem," the man assured her. Then he turned to his friend. "Right, Reed?"

Dr. Atchison grumbled something under his breath that she was fairly certain wasn't an agreement.

"What was that?" Dr. Mahoney asked.

"I said, 'Fine,'" the other man snapped.

Funny, Mindy thought, but it sure hadn't sounded as if he'd said, *Fine.*

"Um, really," she continued hastily, "I don't think I—"

"Of course you do," Dr. Mahoney assured her.

Mindy decided not to dwell on that. "I'm probably going to be working late," she said instead, "and you doubtless have other things to—"

"Not a thing in the world," the blond doctor assured her. "In fact, we've been looking forward to a nice, leisurely meal, haven't we, Reed?"

"Mmm."

Dr. Mahoney smiled at Mindy winningly. "And there you have it."

She opened her mouth to say something else that might excuse her from any further association with these two enigmatic—albeit very attractive and not a little intriguing—men, but Donna returned with their coffee, elbowing Mindy gently out of the way.

"You go sit," the other waitress said. "Get off your feet

for a little while. I'll keep an eye on your tables. The dinner rush is about over, anyway. And you gotta take care of that little bun in your oven.''

Mindy felt herself color at the other waitress's comment. She wrapped her sweater even more tightly around herself, crossing her arms over her lower abdomen as if she might protect the life growing there, even though there was really no threat to that life at all—not at the moment, anyway.

Because she was so small, and because this was her first time being pregnant, she still wasn't showing that much, even though she was five months along. She had hoped the average observer wouldn't notice her condition yet but she supposed she was kidding herself in that. Not that she hadn't told her co-workers at Evie's about it—hey, they deserved to know she'd be incapacitated for a few weeks come April, after all. But she didn't want anyone else, especially total strangers, to know the particulars of her private life.

''Donna,'' she muttered. ''You don't have to broadcast my…condition…to the whole world, you know.''

But Donna only shrugged as she dumped a handful of creamers onto the table. ''It's okay, Min,'' she said. ''These guys know all about it.''

Mindy closed her eyes and felt her cheeks flame brighter. ''Donna…'' she said again. Because these two men probably hadn't noticed her condition before now. The reason they knew about her pregnancy was more than likely because some-one—someone like, oh, say Donna—had told them about it. And seeing as how once you got Donna started, it was really hard to turn her off, Mindy could only imagine what else the other waitress had let slip.

''Oh, come on,'' Donna said. ''It's no big deal, being knocked up and homeless. It happens to a lot of women.''

Mindy raised a hand to cup it over her eyes and closed them tight. ''I was *not* knocked up,'' she said. ''Sam and I made a conscious decision to have a baby. Can I help it if he…'' She sighed heavily, dropped her hand back to her side and strove for a bright smile that she was certain fell short. "Never mind. Just…try not to spread around the particulars, okay? Please?"

Donna shrugged again. "Sure thing, Min." Then she turned to the two men seated at the booth. "Forget I said anything about Mindy's…you know…situation, okay, gents? And please do point out to her that I never told you about what a big drunk her husband was, did I? Or how he slept around on her the whole time they were married? Or how, in my opinion, she's better off without him anyway?"

"It's true," Dr. Mahoney agreed. "She never did tell us about that."

Donna nodded, smugly, Mindy thought. "See? That was private, so I kept that part to myself." She turned back to her two customers. "Your sandwiches should only take a few more minutes."

And with that, Donna spun around and headed back toward the kitchen, leaving Mindy to fend for herself.

"Oooh…" she said, lifting her hand to her forehead again. "I think I'm going to be sick."

"Here, sit down."

She felt two strong hands cup her shoulders and softly urge her forward and was surprised, upon opening her eyes, to see that it was the dark-haired doctor who was doing the gentle cajoling. It seemed like a gesture that would have been more appropriate coming from the man who'd identified himself as Dr. Mahoney. Or perhaps not, she thought further as she let Dr. Atchison sit her down at his place in the booth. He remained standing, hooking his hands on his hips, but he glowered at his friend.

"Now look what you've done," he said.

"What *I've* done?" the other doctor exclaimed. "I didn't do anything. What are you talking about?"

"You've embarrassed her," Dr. Atchison said. "How could you embarrass her like that?"

Dr. Mahoney gaped at him. "I didn't do that. Donna did that."

"But you're the one who started this whole thing, so you're responsible."

"Yeah, but—"

"You should be ashamed of yourself. Taking advantage of a pregnant woman. Just where do you get off?"

"Reed, what the hell has gotten into you? I never—"

"She obviously wants to be left alone, so we ought to just leave her alone."

"But, Reed, she's—"

"A nice girl. You said so yourself. So we should both definitely—"

"*Excuse me!*"

Mindy had to raise her voice when she interrupted, so animated—and loud—had the two men become in their argument. An argument that she seemed to be at the heart of, an argument she didn't for one moment understand, an argument that everyone in Evie's Diner seemed really, really interested in hearing. Thankfully, though, both men ceased at her outburst. Unfortunately, they both turned to stare at her in openmouthed surprise, as if she'd just jumped up onto the table to dance the cha-cha with a rose stuck between her teeth.

She pushed her way out of the booth and stood next to Dr. Atchison, trying not to feel overwhelmed by the fact that he towered over her by at least a foot, and probably weighed twice as much as she did. "If you'll both excuse me," she said, "I have work to do."

"We'll talk later," Dr. Mahoney told her as she turned to go.

"No, we won't," she assured him.

But without missing a beat, he assured her right back, "Oh, yes, Miss…Mindy…we will."

Three

"**O**kay, let me get this straight," Mindy said an hour later as she enjoyed dessert with the two doctors who had suddenly become the center of her universe. She still couldn't quite figure out how she'd been talked into joining them for dessert and coffee—or in her case, dessert and warm milk—after they'd finished their dinner and she'd concluded her shift. Seth—and when had she gotten past referring to them as "Dr."?—had just been so convincing. So charming. So sweet. She hadn't been able to resist him.

Actually, she thought, that wasn't quite true. The one she hadn't been able to resist was Reed. Because in keeping with their utter opposite-ness, as charming and sweet as Seth had been, Reed had seemed—and still did seem—so quiet and withdrawn. Not in a negative way, just…in a thoughtful way. In a resigned way. As if he were contemplating some matter of great importance. Seth, on the other hand, seemed to find the matter—whatever it was—kind of amusing. But it was

Reed's utter concern for something that had drawn Mindy into whatever mystery the two men had created.

But now that mystery was solved, and in solving it, Mindy's confusion was only compounded. So she reiterated what they'd told her in an effort to make some sense of it.

"So, you two made a bet at work earlier that you'd see someone perform a gesture of goodwill this evening," she went on. "Is that right?"

"That's right," Seth confirmed.

"You," she went on, pointing an index finger at him, "thought that the two of you would witness a person performing a gesture of goodwill toward another person. Am I following right?"

"You're following right," Seth agreed.

"And you," she said, pointing now at Reed, "thought there was no way you two would see something like that."

"Yeah, yeah, yeah," Reed grumbled.

Mindy shook her head at him. "Boy, you sure do have a low opinion of the human race."

He gazed down into his coffee cup. "So I've been told. On a number of occasions."

He was glowering again, she noted, but somehow the action seemed insincere. She fought back a smile. She'd never seen someone try so hard to be a malcontent, when it was obvious that malcontentedness was the last thing present inside him. Still, there was no point in puzzling over that quandary, she thought. Not when she had a perfectly good other quandary commanding her attention at the moment.

"So then you guys saw me buy dinner for Mr. McCoy," she said, "and that was the gesture of goodwill that sealed the wager."

"You got it," Seth told her.

"So Reed lost and now he has to pay up by performing a good deed himself."

"Yepper," Seth said enthusiastically.

Mindy switched her attention from one man to the other and back again. "I don't get it."

"Don't get what?" Seth asked. "You just described the situation perfectly."

"But where do I fit in? I mean, aside from having done something nice for someone else, thereby making you the winner of the bet..." She shrugged, then repeated, "Where do I fit in?"

"Well, the least we could do is make sure you're rewarded for your good deed," Seth told her.

"Oh, that's not necessary," she assured him. "I mean, I didn't do it for a reward."

"I know!" Seth exclaimed. "That's what's so great about all this."

"But—"

"You did it because you're such a genuinely good person, and because you felt like it was the right thing to do. And for that, you deserve a reward."

"But—"

"And Reed here is going to reward you."

"But—"

"Just wait till you hear what he's going to do for you," Seth interjected—again—before she had a chance to object— again. "He and I discussed it all through dinner, and you're gonna love this idea. I promise you."

He turned to his companion, who was seated next to Mindy—and no matter how hard she tried to scrunch herself up into the corner of the booth, Reed was still way too close to her—then smiled that game-show-emcee smile again.

And in that voice reminiscent of Bob Barker, he added, "Reed? What's Mindy earned for her good deed?"

Reed sighed heavily, appearing none too happy about the good deed that he was obligated, out of a gambling loss, to perform. When he turned to look at Mindy, his expression punctuated his distaste for the whole thing—she didn't think she'd ever seen a man look more grim. Or, rather, he would have looked grim. If it hadn't been for that telltale glimmer of warmth, and something else akin to hopefulness, that she saw shimmering in his dark eyes.

What an extremely interesting combination of contradictions the man was, she thought. Mindy found herself wishing that she had a chance to investigate him further, wishing that there was some way she might get to know him better. She wished she could find out why he tried so hard to hide what kind of person he really was, why he adopted such a gruff exterior to mask what was obviously a soft center. She wished—

Nothing, she told herself quickly, adamantly. That's what she wished. She wished absolutely nothing. The last thing she needed in her life right now was a curiosity about a man she would never have a chance to investigate further or know better. Because after tonight, he'd be out of her life for good.

And even if, by some wild miracle, their paths crossed again, he wasn't a man for her. She was a pregnant waitress who was barely managing to keep her life together. He was a successful doctor who'd clearly enjoyed every advantage life had to offer.

And even if by some even wilder miracle he took an interest in her, he wasn't her type at all. Not just because of their social and economic differences, but because his attitude toward life in no way mirrored hers. Mindy was the kind of person who looked for the good in others, who hoped for the best, who expected that everything, eventually, would work out. This man clearly felt completely opposite. Even if there might be a spark of hope and a kindling of goodwill deep down inside him, he obviously didn't nurture that tiny flame. He didn't seem to truly believe in it. He didn't act upon it. He and Mindy would never get along.

Like there was any chance of them getting together in the first place, she thought morosely.

He inhaled deeply before speaking, something that brought her attention back to the fore, where it belonged, and Mindy got the definite impression he really wished he was anywhere but there. Then, very quietly, very slowly, very reluctantly, he said, "Since it looks as if you're about to lose your home, I want you to stay at my place."

Mindy couldn't have been more surprised by the offer—
Ha, some offer, she echoed derisively to herself once it settled
in—and she was helpless to hide her reaction. Her mouth
dropped open in amazement, her eyebrows shot right up to
her hairline and she uttered a loud sound of total and utter
disgust.

"You want me to *what?*" she demanded, fairly spitting the
words.

He, in turn, seemed genuinely surprised by her vehement
response. But he repeated, "You can stay at my place. Here
in Cherry Hill. It's like five minutes away from the diner.
You'll be very comfortable there."

For another long moment Mindy only stared at him, unable
to believe what was happening. These guys had seemed so
nice, she thought. So decent. So warm and kind. Was she a
lousy judge of character, or what? Then again, recalling the
kind of man she had married, was she really surprised that
she'd been so easily duped by these two?

Boy, this was what happened when a person looked for the
good in everybody and always expected the best, she thought
further. She got herself slapped silly by the fates.

She mentally counted to ten before she said anything more,
in an effort to halt her rising temper. "Oh, I get it," she finally
said, proud of herself for somehow managing to keep her voice
level. "No good deed goes unpunished, right? I did something
nice for someone and now I have to pay for it, is that it?"

It was clearly not the reaction Reed had been expecting,
because he reared his head back some and frowned in clear
confusion. "What are you talking about?" he asked. "Pay for
it? I thought I was offering you something you need. What's
the problem?"

"Something I need?" she echoed, incredulous. "Hey, the
last thing I need is for some guy to be looking to make me
his…his…" She swallowed with some difficulty. "His kept
woman," she finished in a lower voice, proud of herself again
for finding a term that was socially acceptable—sort of—for
what he was proposing.

He eyed her with confusion again. "Kept woman?" he repeated. "What on earth are you…?"

His question trailed off at a bark of laughter that erupted from the other side of the table. When Mindy turned to look at Seth, she saw him fighting back laughter—with a tremendous amount of effort but without much success.

"What's so funny?" she asked.

"You," he replied without compunction, barely restraining his chuckles. "Thinking that Reed wants you to be his…his…his kept woman." He punctuated the observation with another ripple of laughter. "Oh, that's rich. Wait'll they hear about that one at the hospital. I can't wait to tell the nurses in CCU."

Now Mindy was really confused. She turned her attention from Seth to Reed, only to find the latter growing red in the face. Really red. For a moment, she thought the reaction was caused by his anger and outrage. Then, suddenly, she realized he was embarrassed.

"Uh…isn't that what you were proposing?" she asked.

Seth laughed harder, and Reed grew redder. "No," he finally said, not looking at her. "That wasn't what I was proposing at all."

"Then what?"

"I apologize, Miss Harmon—"

"Mindy," she corrected him automatically.

He dipped his head forward to acknowledge that he had heard her but he still continued, "Miss Harmon. I suppose I should have phrased my offer a little differently."

"Yeah, I'll say," Seth remarked, still chuckling. "Oh, that's a good one. Reed having a kept woman in his apartment. Why 'keep' one when there are plenty pounding on the door to get in and take advantage of him? Hey, I can name a half dozen nurses right now who'd like to keep *him* in *their* apartments. Man, oh, man, I think this is the funniest thing I've ever heard in my life."

Reed wished he could share Seth's point of view, but frankly, what Mindy had said was the most humiliating thing he'd ever heard in his life. She thought he intended to set her up at his place and take advantage of her sexually? *Her?* A pregnant woman? A pregnant woman on the rebound? Just how lonely and desperate did she think he was?

As quickly as the question formed in his head, Reed shoved it aside. He wasn't lonely *or* desperate, he assured himself, no matter what she seemed to think. Nor was he the kind of sicko creep who would use a woman in Mindy's situation and condition to satisfy his own longings. She was right, he thought. No good deed went unpunished.

"What I meant, Miss Harmon," he began again, "is that, even though I live just outside Philadelphia myself—*west* of Philadelphia, I might add—I have a condo here in Cherry Hill that I keep for those occasions when I work late or get snowed in or what have you. Ninety percent of the time it's empty. Donna gave us the impression that you don't have any other family you might be able to stay with—"

"No, I don't. But that's really none of your—"

"Then there's no reason why you shouldn't take advantage of my condo. Until you find a new apartment of your own, I mean. This time of year, it's got to be difficult to find a place to live, and you might very well wind up having to put your things in storage, so—"

"I rent a furnished apartment," she interrupted him. "I have very few things to store. That's not likely to be a problem."

"Okay," he went on, "but it still must be difficult looking for a place this time of year."

"Yes," she agreed. "It has been. Frankly, I'm not sure I *will* find a place by the time I need to be out of my apartment. But something will turn up," she assured him halfheartedly. "It always does."

He hesitated only a moment before asking, "What if it doesn't?"

Mindy glanced down at the backs of her hands, unable to meet his gaze. "I'll worry about that when…if…it happens."

"It *won't* happen if you take advantage of my condo,"

he pointed out. ''And there's absolutely no reason why you shouldn't.''

She turned to gaze at him for a long, thoughtful moment, a moment when Reed felt himself being pulled more and more deeply into the pale-green depths of her eyes. Finally, softly, she replied, ''Actually, there's a very good reason why I shouldn't stay at your condo.''

''I can't imagine what it would be.''

''The other ten percent of the time,'' she said.

He narrowed his eyes in confusion. ''I'm sorry, I don't follow you.''

''You say the place is empty ninety percent of the time,'' she reminded him.

''Yes. So?''

''So that means that ten percent of the time, it's not empty. You're living there.''

''Well, it goes without saying that I wouldn't use it if you were in residence. I'd just go ahead and make the drive home, or I could stay at a hotel.''

''He could stay with me,'' Seth piped up.

But neither Reed nor Mindy—Miss Harmon—were listening to him. Instead, they were utterly focused on each other, something that made a ripple of errant heat indolently wind through Reed's entire body. With no small effort he shook off the sensation.

''I...um... It...it's not necessary,'' she finally stammered. ''Thank you anyway, but I don't think it's a good idea.''

For the life of him, Reed couldn't figure out why it hurt to hear her turn down his offer. But it *did* hurt. Like a dull ache deep inside him that thumped against his heart. He'd never felt such a sensation before. And he didn't like it at all. What he liked even less was the expression on Mindy's face, the look of discomfort and uneasiness that he felt somehow responsible for rousing.

''Really, Miss Harmon,'' he tried again, ''it would be no trouble at all. You'd be doing me a favor, because I would rest easier knowing there's someone there.''

"Yeah and it's a nice place," Seth threw in, more soberly this time, as if he, too, sensed the sudden change in mood that surrounded them. "He's got a big-screen TV, huge eat-in kitchen, full bar…well, not that you'll be needing *that*. Not unless you want to throw a party or something."

"Thank you," she said, still not looking at either of them. "But it's not necessary. If you feel compelled to do a good deed, Dr. Atchison—"

"Reed," he corrected her.

"—Dr. Atchison, then I suggest you volunteer some of your time to a local charity that could use it. Me, I can take care of myself."

As if wanting to emphasize that part of her statement, Mindy glanced up again, throwing her head back fiercely, eyeing him levelly, as if daring him to contradict her.

Oh, God, he wished he could find the words to do just that. Because if there was one solid, unequivocal truth in the world, it was that Mindy Harmon needed somebody right now. Badly. And Reed just couldn't understand why she would refuse to allow someone into her life who could help her out.

"Now, if you'll excuse me," she said, "the last bus runs in about fifteen minutes, so I need to be going."

"Please, Miss Harmon," Reed said, "the least I can do is give you a ride home."

"No, thank you," she said with a swift shake of her head. "I'll be fine. On my own."

He wasn't sure, but he thought she added a little more emphasis to those last three words than was really necessary, as if she were saying them to convince herself of their truth more than she was him. Still, there was little he could do but respect her wishes. If she didn't want to accept a helping hand, there was no way he could force the issue. Seth would just have to accept some other gesture of goodwill to settle the debt. Because Miss Mindy Harmon wasn't going to be it.

Without further comment, Reed scooted out of the booth to enable her exit—though, as he watched her more closely, he decided *escape* might be a more appropriate word—and she took advantage of his action to immediately push herself out behind him, as if she feared he would try to stop her.

"Thank you for dessert," she said softly when she was standing again. "That more than settles your debt, in my opinion, Dr. Atchison. It was a nice thing for you to do."

Without a further word, she spun around and walked away. Reed and Seth both remained silent as she left, never once looking back over her shoulder at either of them.

And Reed couldn't quite help himself as he settled his hands on his hips once more, leveled an angry look on his best friend and said, "See what happens when you look for the best in people? You get kicked right in the teeth."

His words came back to haunt him less than a half hour later as he stood in the living room of his Cherry Hill condo. The one that was only minutes away from the diner where Mindy Harmon worked, the one he'd thought would be the perfect solution to her current predicament.

Really, he told himself now, he hadn't been kicked in the teeth. He'd just kind of been elbowed in the gut a little. Well, maybe more than an elbow. And maybe more than a little. But not quite a punch. That dull ache near his heart had just sort of spread down into his belly, and something told him it wouldn't be going away any time soon.

And, really, he hadn't been correct in his assessment that his place would be suitable for Mindy, either, he thought as he further surveyed his surroundings. Although he'd always considered the condo comfortable enough, when all was said and done he'd never actually paid that much attention to it. He'd always pretty much considered it to be a temporary refuge of sorts, a place where he could stay on those occasions when he couldn't—or didn't want to—make it back to the old homestead in Ardmore.

But now as he studied his home away from home more critically, he realized it wasn't much of a home at all, in spite of the lushness of the furnishings, which were certainly very nice. And very expensive—he'd hired one of Philadelphia's premier decorators to do the place up right. A cognac-colored leather sofa and wing chairs topped an Oriental rug of rich jewel tones. The walls were painted a dark hunter green that bled to what the decorator had called "sage" in the kitchen. The bedroom beyond was a dusky berry color, the bathroom dark blue. The whole place was dark, come to think of it, he noted for the first time. He fought off the urge to switch on more than the single standing lamp he'd illuminated upon entering.

How could he think this place would be appropriate for Mindy? he asked himself. She was so full of light, so airy, so sublime. His dark, formal, soulless condo would totally overwhelm her. There was no warmth here, no light. What on earth had he been thinking to even suggest she would be comfortable here?

And how had he ever been comfortable here himself?

Of course, the answer to that was simple. He never *had* been comfortable here, not really. But then, he'd never much been comfortable anywhere, so that hadn't bothered him. As empty and isolated as the condo felt to him, the house in Ardmore was more so, only on a much larger scale. Then again, that was really no surprise, either. Reed was, after all, empty and isolated on a large scale, too. It was a family tradition.

He sighed fitfully, running a restless hand through his dark hair. In spite of his misgivings, and as inappropriate as the condo seemed for Mindy, it was still a damned sight better than the streets. It might not be a bad idea to lay in a few groceries, he thought. Nothing perishable, of course, just something to have on hand. Just in case. If nothing else, they'd probably start seeing some serious snow before long. December was already proving to be colder—and had seen more precipitation—than usual. He never knew when he'd have to work late and might have trouble getting home one night. No sense in waiting until the last minute to get the place ready.

You just never knew what might happen.

* * *

Mindy hummed "Frosty the Snowman" under her breath as she wiped the last remnants of the lunch rush off the counter at Evie's two afternoons following what she had almost convinced herself was a dream—the episode in which two handsome doctors had made veiled offers of…of…of something she had yet to adequately identify. As if triggered by the memory, the hairs on the back of her neck suddenly leaped to attention, in exactly the same way they had that night, right around the time she'd made the acquaintance of Drs. Atchison and Mahoney.

Glancing up from her task, she saw Reed—Dr. Atchison, she hastily corrected herself—ambling forward, alone. So. It was he, and not Seth Mahoney, who was responsible for the leaping neck hairs, she mused. Funny, but somehow she wasn't the least bit surprised by the realization.

His gaze never left her face as he strode easily forward, approaching a stool immediately in front of her. And she couldn't quite keep from noticing how very handsome he was. It had started snowing again that morning. Soft, negligent flakes of white clung to his dark hair, sparkling like tiny gems. His long overcoat of charcoal wool hung open over a suit just a shade darker, making him look like an ad for something extremely expensive in *GQ* magazine.

She stilled the motion of her hand as he drew nearer and sat down, but her heart rate jumped to double time at his closeness. Surely she only imagined the warmth that surrounded her at his nearness, and the scent of something musky and masculine that accompanied it. Surely she only imagined the spark of heat in his dark eyes and the hint of a genuine smile that played about his lips. And surely she only imagined the leap of delight that swirled up from somewhere deep inside her at seeing him again.

Still staring at her, he shrugged off his heavy coat and settled it on the stool beside him. Only then did Mindy notice that his necktie depicted none other than the Grinch himself. She couldn't help but smile. He sure did go out of his way to remind the world at large that he was nothing but a big ol' humbug. Really, she thought, she probably shouldn't get such a warm, fuzzy feeling inside when faced with a humbug. Nevertheless, warm and fuzzy—among other sensations—just so happened to be exactly what Reed…or rather, Dr. Atchison…aroused in her.

No, no, no, not *aroused,* she hastily corrected herself. That wasn't the right word to use at all. No way did he *arouse* her. Uh-uh. Never in a million years. She was a pregnant woman about to be tossed out of her home on her keister. The last thing she needed to be feeling these days was aroused by some guy she'd just met.

No, surely what Reed—Dr. Atchison…oh, what the heck…Reed—did was, um…oh, gosh…inspire her. Yeah, that was it. Pregnant women were always experiencing feelings of inspiration, weren't they? And hey, it was Christmas, after all. A very inspirational time of year. So it was *inspiration* she felt when faced with Reed Atchison. Inspiration, not arousal. He *inspired* her.

Yeah, that's the ticket.

"Hello," she said, trying to shove the clutter of her thoughts aside, and not succeeding very well. "Long time, no see."

"How are you feeling?" he asked, his voice laced with a concern that no stranger should be feeling for her. Somehow, though, Mindy sensed that his concern was, in fact, genuine. "You seemed to be a little off your game the other night."

That was an understatement, she thought. She'd been utterly exhausted the other night. And not much had changed since then.

"Not that Seth and I made things any better for you," he added. "We could have eased into our explanation a little better. Again, I apologize for giving you the wrong impression."

She lifted a shoulder and quickly let it drop. "No harm done," she told him.

Somehow, though, she knew that wasn't quite true. She realized she'd hurt his feelings when she'd turned down his offer of a place to stay, but honestly, what else was she supposed to have done? Accept it? Not likely.

Mindy may have made some dumb mistakes in her life but at least she'd learned from them. And the last thing she was going to do was trust a total stranger or rush into a friendship—or any other kind of *-ship*—with a man she barely knew. The last time she'd done that, she'd wound up married to a man who had been nothing but trouble, a man who had left her far worse off than she'd ever been in her life. She was better off alone.

Impulsively, she dropped her hand to her belly, opening her palm over her softly swollen womb. Then again, she thought warmly, she wasn't quite alone, was she? And maybe, in one way at least, Sam hadn't left her so badly off.

"So how *are* you feeling?"

She glanced up at the question and marveled again that a man who barely knew her could be so worried about her. But worried he clearly was. "I'm okay," she told him. "I think I might be coming down with a cold, but nothing major."

He frowned. "In your condition, that could very well be something major. There have been studies linking dyslexic children to mothers who contracted the flu or a common cold while they were pregnant."

Oh, fine, she thought. This from a doctor. As if she didn't have enough to worry about just being pregnant. "No, it's just a few sniffles," she insisted. "I'll be perfectly all right. Honest."

He didn't look convinced. "How many hours a week are you working?"

She was unable to stop the incredulous little sound that escaped her. But her voice was mild as she asked, "What is this? The Spanish Inquisition?"

He lifted his hands, palm out, as if in surrender. "I'm sorry. You're right. It's none of my business."

"Exactly," she told him. Then, feeling as if she really needed to hammer that home, she added with much insistence, "I can take care of myself."

His dark eyes somehow grew darker. "So you've said. Several times."

"Because it's true."

"Fine," he relented, reaching for one of the menus tucked between the ketchup bottle and the sugar shaker. "I'll just, um, order lunch," he added. "That is, after all, the reason I came by."

Mindy nodded curtly. "Can I get you a cup of coffee or something?"

"Coffee would be great," he said, not looking up from the menu.

Immediately, she fled to the big coffee urn at the other end of the counter, feeling significantly more winded when she got there than a dozen strides—however quickly taken—warranted. She began to feel a bit dizzy, so she closed her eyes, gripped the counter and inhaled a few deep breaths, releasing them slowly, one by one. After a moment, when she felt steadier, she opened her eyes again, only to find Reed down at the other end of the counter staring at her. Hard. So, with one more deep sigh, she filled a cup of coffee and carried it—slowly—back to him.

"Are you sure you're okay?" he asked as she set it down before him.

"I'm fine," she lied.

"Because you look a little pale to me."

She lifted her chin a fraction. "Is that your informed medical opinion, Doctor?"

He lifted one corner of his mouth into what might have been a smile, but she wasn't sure. "Uh, yes," he said. "As a matter of fact, it is."

She deflated some. "Oh. I, um, I just have a really fair complexion, that's all," she said, not quite looking at him.

"I also noticed," he continued, "as a physician, mind you, that you seemed to be on the verge of passing out down there a second ago."

"I just stumbled a little bit," she told him. "Took me a minute to steady myself." Then, before he could offer any more informed medical opinions, she hurried on, "Have you decided what you'd like to order?"

When he didn't reply immediately, Mindy braved a glance up at him. He opened his mouth to say something that she was pretty sure wasn't going to be a lunch order, then surprised her by stating, "I'll have the steak sandwich, please. Medium-rare. With french fries."

She scribbled the words down without really seeing them and, after a silent nod to Reed, turned to clip the order to the wheel at the kitchen window, calling out halfheartedly, "Order in, Pete."

"Seriously, Miss Harmon, how many hours a week do you work?"

For some reason, Mindy wasn't surprised that he asked the question again. And for some reason, she no longer felt reluctant to respond to it. Somehow, she knew he wouldn't leave it alone until he had an answer, anyway. "I don't know," she said softly. "Fifty or sixty, I guess."

"Fifty or sixty?" he echoed, not even bothering to mask his outrage. "No wonder you look so tired. You shouldn't be on your feet that much. Not in your condition."

She lifted her chin a fraction in defiance, then realized the gesture was probably pointless. Defiant was the last thing she was feeling these days. She was way too tired to feel defiant. "When it gets closer to my due date, I'm not going to be able to work as many hours as I can now," she explained. "So I need to work while I'm physically able. I try to pick up extra shifts here and there when I can."

"Physically able," he repeated blandly. But he said nothing more to clarify what he meant.

"Look, it's none of your business," she told him again, less adamantly this time. When she met his gaze, she had intended for it to be with a steely determination. But his eyes were just so dark, so warm and so very, very worried that she crumpled under the weight of her anxiety—her anxiety and his, too. "I mean, I appreciate your concern," she said, easing up some, "but truly, it's just…" She scrunched up her shoulders and let them drop again. "It's none of your concern."

He didn't surrender this time when she offered her assurance. Instead, he looked even less convinced than he had before. "If you're so pressed for money," he said, "then how come you dipped into your precious resources to buy dinner for that man the other night?"

"*That man* has a name," she said pointedly.

He shifted uncomfortably on his seat. "I know. I just can't remember what it was."

"Mr. McCoy."

"Fine. Mr. McCoy. If you're so strapped financially, why did you buy him dinner?"

She expelled another incredulous little sound. "Because he didn't have enough to buy it for himself."

"And you did?"

"Well, yeah."

He seemed to be waiting for a fuller explanation, but Mindy had no idea what more to say.

"That's it?" he asked. "You bought the guy dinner because you had money and he didn't?"

She nodded.

"But you can barely afford to feed yourself."

"Barely, yeah," she conceded. "But I can afford it. He can't. He needed a hand. I was able to give it to him. It's no big deal."

"No big deal?" he echoed in disbelief.

"Hey, if everybody lent a helping hand now and then, there probably wouldn't be any people out there who needed a helping hand."

"Yes, but—"

"Order up, Mindy!"

She muttered an "Excuse me" to Reed and scooped up her tray to make her rounds. By the time she got back to the counter, Reed had received his own lunch and was picking at it without much enthusiasm.

"Is everything okay?" she asked.

He started to nod, then immediately switched to shaking his head. "No, everything is *not* okay," he said, glancing up to meet her gaze levelly. "You're a nice person who's had a lot of misfortune dumped on her lately and who's still getting dumped on. You'll do nice things for other people but you won't let other people do nice things for you. That makes no sense to me."

After a brief hesitation that she spent trying to understand why he was so upset—and why such a warm ripple of pleasure wound through her at his insistence that she was so nice—all Mindy could manage in reply was, "I am *not* moving into your apartment, and that's final."

He expelled a single, humorless chuckle. "Why not? It would be the perfect arrangement for you."

"It's not necessary," she stated adamantly. "I'll be just fine. I barely know you. I'm certainly not your responsibility."

"That's beside the point. It doesn't matter if you barely know me. I—"

"That's exactly the point," she interrupted him. "I *don't* know you. And I'm *not* your responsibility. Period."

He eyed her warily. "Then I guess, Miss Harmon... Mindy...that we'll just have to get to know each other better, won't we?"

Four

Reed had no idea what caused him to make such a remark. The last thing he needed to be doing right now was get to know a pregnant diner waitress better. The words had just sort of…popped out, that was all. He hadn't been able to help himself.

But once uttered, he was surprised to discover that he really didn't want to take the comment back. What was the harm in getting to know Mindy better? he asked himself. She was a sweet person and she seemed to be utterly alone in the world. Much like himself. Well, not the sweet part, of course. God knew the last adjective that should be applied to Reed Atchison was *sweet*. But the alone part… Well, they definitely seemed to have that in common. In spades.

She seemed to have no idea what to make of his offer, however, because she only stared at him in what appeared to be truly baffled silence. She still suspected his motives, he realized. She was still under the impression that he wanted to take advantage of her.

Then again, he supposed he couldn't blame her for that. She didn't seem to have had too many breaks in life. Her husband had been a drunk and a louse, according to the illustrious Donna. She'd already lost one home in the last year and now she was about to lose another. He guessed if life beat you down long enough, you learned not to trust much of anything. Or anybody.

So then what's your excuse, pal?

The question erupted in Reed's mind out of nowhere. It was true that he hadn't exactly been beaten down by life, he supposed. He'd been born into a wealthy family, had received every privilege a human being could receive, had known nothing but good fortune since day one. Yet he mistrusted life more than anyone. Certainly more than Mindy did, if her penchant for buying dinners she couldn't afford for other people, and that little plastic Santa Claus pinned to her sweater, were any indication.

Guiltily, Reed glanced down at his Grinch necktie and grimaced.

"Your sandwich is going to get cold if you don't eat it."

When he glanced up again, it was to find Miss Mindy Harmon studying him with an expression he couldn't quite identify. She seemed not to have heard his declaration that they should get to know each other better, and, at the moment, he was wondering if maybe he'd even said it out loud. Could be he'd only been thinking about it and hadn't actually put voice to the desire. Hopefully, that was the case. Because he was beginning to feel as if some kind of strange madness was descending upon him. That could be the only explanation for the odd, maudlin, sappy course his thoughts seemed to be traveling lately.

Picking up his sandwich, Reed took a healthy bite and chewed. Funny how tasteless the thing was, seeing as how the food at Evie's was supposed to be so good. It hadn't been all that great the other night, either, he recalled, even though Seth had raved about it all through dinner. Funnier still was how his appetite had absolutely fled. He'd been starving when he'd come into the diner. Lunch really had been foremost in his mind, really had been his reason for coming. Hadn't it?

Of course it had.

Mindy Harmon was just incidental to it all, he told himself. He'd be better off if he remembered that.

He washed the flavorless swallow down with an even more flavorless sip of his coffee and watched her while she worked. There was a surprisingly elegant efficiency to her movements, and she was clearly more than comfortable performing her job. She'd obviously been doing this kind of thing for a long time. She seemed to know a good number of her customers well and she laughed often with them. There was a warmth and kindness about her that he sensed was utterly inbred. Nobody could fake that much niceness.

He wondered about her husband then, about what kind of idiot would cheat on a woman like her. And he wondered what there had been about the man that Mindy had fallen in love with, why she had chosen him as the one with whom she wanted to grow old.

There was no accounting for taste, he thought. And love—at least from what he'd heard, having never experienced it himself—was a capricious thing. All the more reason to avoid it, he thought now. Because if someone like Mindy could have lost her heart to a man who didn't deserve it, then who was to say the same thing wouldn't happen to Reed?

Not that his heart was up for grabs anyway, he reminded himself. Nor was it in any danger of being swept up by anyone, deserving or not. The Main Line Atchisons didn't fall in love. When they married, it was out of convenience—for financial, political or professional reasons. That was the way it had always been. That was the way it would always stay.

Even in his own generation, all the Atchison marriages were voluntarily arranged according to where the union would be the most paramount, the most productive, the most profitable. Oh, his various cousins might insist that they truly loved the people with whom they walked down the aisle, but it's funny how all those weddings benefited the family as a whole. Funny how all of them seemed more like sound investments than they did loving unions.

And that was why Reed would remain a single man. He was just fine financially, politically and professionally, thank you very much. And love, it went without saying, would never be a part of his emotional landscape. It would be pointless and cruel to unite himself with a woman who would no doubt want and need—and deserve—so much more than fiscal soundness.

So, really, what was the point?

His thoughts were thankfully interrupted when Mindy returned, toting a coffee carafe in each hand and looking as if she was about to collapse. His instincts screamed at him to get up off his duff and make her go home to lie down, whether she liked it or not, but he knew such a reaction would only make her mad. She wasn't any of his business, he reminded himself. She'd told him that often enough, and deep down inside he knew that was true.

But, dammit, she needed help. Her pregnancy was obviously a difficult one, draining her of her energy and strength. If she kept up this pace, it would be downright unhealthy. She might even lose the baby if she didn't take better care of herself.

"Are you seeing a doctor?" he asked. The question erupted from his mouth before he could stop it, and it came out sounding harsher than he'd intended.

Evidently, Mindy thought so, too, because she jerked around at the sound of it, sloshing some of the coffee over the lip of the carafe and onto her hand. The hot beverage must have burned her pretty badly, because, instinctively, she released the handle and the glass container went crashing to the ground. Naturally, she jumped back as it fell, but not far enough to keep the coffee from splashing her legs. When it did, she cried out her pain at being burned and dropped the other carafe, too, repeating the entire process all over again.

The second pot was just hitting the ground when Reed leaped over the countertop, the hot coffee in that pot burning what little of Mindy hadn't been burned already. And without thinking about what he was doing, he scooped her up into his arms. She must have been hurting pretty badly because she didn't even object. She only circled his neck with both arms and burst into tears.

Quickly, he surveyed the damage, but because she was wearing tights he couldn't tell how badly she'd been burned. An elderly woman appeared beside him then, a skinny, white-haired, yellow-uniformed fireball.

"Is she okay?" the woman asked, her voice gravelly and urgent.

"I don't know," Reed said. "We need to get her out of her tights. I'm a doctor," he hastened to add.

"I'm Evie," the woman told him. "Bring her back to my office."

"I'd rather take her to the hospital," he said. But already he was following Evie toward the kitchen. They did need to get her out of her tights and they needed to get some ice on her legs. Once they'd done that, Reed was taking her over to Seton General. And he would *not* take no for an answer.

Not this time.

"I *told* you I was fine."

Mindy couldn't quite keep the smugness from her voice—though smug was pretty much the last thing she felt as she sat on a gurney in examining room C of the Seton General Hospital emergency room. Having to clutch closed a paper-thin hospital gown as tightly as one could behind oneself sort of left one feeling anything but smug. For all the good it did. She could still feel a steady—and cold—breeze blowing from somewhere behind her. That didn't bother her nearly as much as what was in front of her, though—Reed Atchison. He was seated on a stool, examining her bare legs, and Mindy didn't think she'd ever be able to look at her knees quite the same way again.

"First-degree burns on a pregnant woman isn't what I'd call fine," he muttered without diverting his attention from one particularly red area on her left shin. "You're lucky this isn't any worse than it is."

"I'm lucky workman's comp will cover the ER bills," she mumbled to herself.

He glanced up and frowned. "What?"

"Nothing," she muttered.

He eyed her narrowly for a moment, then returned his attention to her legs. Her bare legs. Her bare, winter-white legs. Her bare, winter-white, bony chicken legs. She sighed heavily. She scarcely recognized her own body these days. Between the changes wrought by pregnancy and all the weight she'd lost after Sam's death, there was little of her left to recognize. A year ago she'd been fifteen pounds heavier and in the glowing pink of health. These days she looked more like a scarecrow. A scarecrow with a little pot belly, at any rate.

Even after five months of being pregnant, she'd only gained six pounds. She knew it should be a lot more than that, knew she should have filled out considerably better than she had. But between coping with Sam's death and her severe morning sickness during her first trimester, she'd scarcely been able to keep anything down. And these days she worked so many shifts at the diner, she didn't have *time* to gain weight.

A little ripple of fear bubbled up inside her at the knowledge that she wasn't in as good a shape as she should be. She wanted to do what was best for her unborn child, wanted to make sure the baby was as healthy and robust as it could possibly be. She wanted to give it all the nutrition, rest and contentment she could, even while it was still growing in her womb. *Especially* while it was growing in her womb.

But she knew she wasn't doing a very good job of that. She should be taking better care of herself, she thought, not for the first time. She should be getting some rest and not working so much. She should be eating more and exercising in small doses. But how else was she supposed to provide for herself and her baby after its birth if she didn't make some money *now?*

The thoughts spiraling through her brain brought tears to

her eyes, compounding what was already an embarrassing, un-comfortable situation. Below her, Reed inspected with much care the last of her wounds, his fingers gentle, his touch almost tender. A sizzle of heat wound up her leg, pooling in her womb before easing up to her heart. She couldn't remember the last time anyone had touched her this way, with simple human kindness. Sam hadn't been exactly the hugging, affec-tionate type. And those times when he'd been drinking, he'd scarcely looked her way at all. Certainly he hadn't given her the physical affection she had longed for.

Then again, nobody in her life really had. Her mother hadn't been overly physical in her gestures of love, either. Oh, she'd told Mindy often enough that she loved her. And there had been smiles and other gestures to reinforce that. But on those occasions when Mindy had tried to embrace her mother, she'd been met with resistance. A quick, awkward hug, a pat on the back, and that would be the end of it.

She curled her fingers over her belly and stroked slowly. Her son or daughter would never feel a lack of affection, she promised herself. And her child would certainly never feel unloved. Once they settled that baby in her arms, Mindy wasn't going to put the little sweetie down ever again. She would hold the infant close, brush tender kisses over its downy soft hair, nuzzle its soft baby skin and hold on with all her heart. Forever and ever and ever.

And speaking of her heart.... It started doing some *very* funny things when Reed ran his palm up along her calf, behind her knee, to the back of her thigh. "Wh-what are you doing?" she stammered, trying to pull free. But he only tightened his grip. "The coffee didn't hit me there."

"Just checking," he said. But his voice, too, sounded a bit ragged and uncertain. "That was a big splash that hit you. It even reached a couple of places on your arm, but they don't look as if they require any special attention."

Mindy dropped her gaze to her forearm and, sure enough, saw an angry red, crescent-shaped mark there, too.

"I'm going to prescribe some antibiotic cream for your

legs,'' he said, his voice returning to Marcus Welby mode as he released her. ''But I think you'll be okay.''

Once again, smugness crept into her voice when she replied, ''I told you so.''

''Nevertheless,'' he added, looking up to fix her with a gaze that was very serious indeed, ''I want you to stay off your feet for a few days.''

''What?''

''I mean it, Mindy. I'm going to call Evie and tell her you are *not* to work for three days.''

''But that's ridiculous,'' she objected. ''You just said yourself that I'm okay.''

''I said you'll *be* okay. After you've been off your feet for a few days. You can't be too careful with burns. Besides, you could use the rest for other reasons, too,'' he added pointedly.

So that was it, she thought. He wanted her to take it easy because of the baby, not the burns. Then again, hadn't she just told herself she needed to slow down? At least she wouldn't be missing any weekend hours. Still, the lunch shift could be pretty profitable during the week.

''Workman's comp may cover your lost wages,'' he said, as if he'd read her thoughts. ''But even if it doesn't, you need to take these three days. Doctor's orders, Mindy. I'm serious. And I'll be checking up on you, just to make sure you obey them.''

By *checking up on you,* Mindy had thought Reed meant that he'd be stopping by the diner everyday to make sure she wasn't working. So she was more than a little surprised when, that very evening, he showed up at her front door. Carrying two brown paper sacks. And looking really, really gorgeous. Faded, snug jeans hugged his long legs and firm thighs and a weathered leather bomber jacket hung open over a tobacco-colored sweater. His dark hair had been gently ruffled by the winter wind, his cheeks stained red by the cold.

Involuntarily, she reached up to tug self-consciously at the scraggly ponytail atop her head, then glanced down at her own attire—a pair of baggy black sweatpants and an *extremely* oversize red sweatshirt, emblazoned with the name of a high school other than the one from which she'd graduated. She'd picked up the garment—and others like it—for fifty cents at a garage sale, knowing she'd need maternity clothes soon and would be unable to afford anything retail. Somehow, remembering that now—and glancing back up at Reed in his expensive designer duds—made her feel like a charity case.

And the two brown sacks he held in his arms only reinforced that feeling. He'd brought her groceries, she realized as the heat of embarrassment wound through her entire body. In spite of all her assurances to the contrary, he still didn't think she could take care of herself. Then again, she thought further, was that really so surprising? Lately, in a lot of ways, she was inclined to agree with him on that score.

Having absolutely no idea what to say to him, she blurted the first thing that popped into her head. "Gee, most guys would bring a woman flowers for a first date."

He smiled at that, a knowing, almost predatory smile. She felt her own cheeks growing redder than his were, though her own reaction was in no way a result of any chill in the air. On the contrary, heat flashed in her belly again and spread fast through her entire system at the expression on his face.

"Is this our first date?" he asked mildly. "Funny, I don't recall asking you out."

"Uh…" she replied eloquently, her utter embarrassment tying her tongue in a knot.

"I mean, I thought about asking you out," he added, the revelation shocking her from the top of her head to the tips of her toes, "but I didn't think you'd say yes if I did."

Oh, boy, Mindy thought. Now she was *really* getting hot. From her embarrassment, of course, she assured herself. No way could it be from anything other than that. "Uh…" she tried again.

"So imagine my delight now to realize now that we are, in fact, dating." The smile that punctuated his sentiment was a cryptic one, and she couldn't tell whether he was kidding or not. Surely, he was, she told herself. Because there was no way a man like him would ever ask out a woman like her. It just didn't happen.

"Uh..." she tried one more time. Finally, her vocabulary kicked back in. "I-it was just a-a little joke," she stammered. "I was, uh, I was only kidding."

His smile changed not one iota. "Were you?"

She didn't quite trust her voice not to betray her, so Mindy only nodded weakly.

"Oh. Then I guess it's a good thing I didn't bring flowers," he said. "Instead, I brought dinner."

She arched her eyebrows in surprise. "You're going to cook for me?"

He shook his head. "Oh, God, no. I don't cook. Ever. I'm a lousy cook. What I do exceptionally well, however, is carryout, so that's what I brought. Hope you like Chinese."

Gosh, Mindy thought, that telltale aroma of soy and teriyaki that suddenly seemed to be overtaking her in waves probably should have clued her off right away. It was just that she'd had her mind, and her nose, evidently—not to mention her eyes, her libido and everything else—on other things at the time. Like how yummy Reed Atchison looked—and smelled. Though, come to think of it, she mused, he did smell a lot like...soy and teriyaki.

"I like Chinese," she said. "But I'm really not all that hungry. Sorry you came all this way for nothing. Thanks, anyway."

She hoped that by standing her ground—her ground being meager at best, seeing as how she took up considerably less of the threshold than he did—and by not issuing an invitation, he'd get the not-so-subtle hint. But he only continued to smile that enigmatic smile, shifting his weight from one foot to the other, without comment.

Mindy sighed heavily. "Oh, all right," she conceded grudgingly, moving to the side. Man, she was *such* a pushover when it came to gorgeous, articulate, sexy, smart, hot, firm-thighed, teriyaki-scented, uh… When it came to attractive males. "You can come in."

She didn't have to ask him twice. The moment she stepped aside, he moved forward, taking up what little of the threshold she hadn't covered herself, and then some. Before she could jump completely out of the way to avoid touching him, he brushed past her and, somehow, he seemed to slow down when he did. The brief contact with his body was actually negligible—just a quick nudge, if that—but somehow it felt like the detonation of an atomic bomb. If Mindy had thought she was hot before…

Oh, boy.

"You didn't have to stop by to check up on me," she said, telling herself she only imagined the breathlessness that seemed to have overtaken her voice. "You could have just picked up the phone and called."

He turned as she closed the door behind him. "Actually, I did call you. Or rather, I *tried.* But the electronic voice that answered told me your line had been disconnected."

She nibbled her lip a little anxiously. "Oh."

"I assume that's because of your landlord's plan to evict everyone from the building, and not because you've had any trouble paying your phone bill recently."

"Mmm," she murmured noncommittally, wondering why she didn't feel more insulted by his intimation that she'd been a bit remiss in paying her bills lately. Probably, she thought, it was because she'd been a bit remiss in paying her bills lately. So what he was saying was actually founded in fact and therefore shouldn't be considered insulting. Or something like that.

At her lack of a response, Reed frowned. "Mindy?" he asked, his expression wary.

She strove to keep her own expression bland. "Yes?"

"*Have* you been having trouble paying your phone bills?"

"Um," she began, "I, uh… Well… No more trouble than I've had paying any other bills," she told him, proud of herself for her unwavering honesty.

But he clearly wasn't buying it.

"Okay, so there were a few months when I was a little late," she confessed. "Those few months were just unfortunately…you know…in a row."

She'd hurried over those last words to finish as quietly as she could, but it hadn't been quietly enough, evidently. Because Reed frowned at her with much disappointment.

"I mailed a check two days ago," she told him. "It obviously just hasn't arrived yet, that's all."

This time he was the one to murmur a noncommittal "Mmm."

"The kitchen is that way," she said, pointing behind him, hoping her comment might steer them onto a safer—and more bland—subject.

As if he couldn't have figured that out by himself, she thought further. Her "kitchen" consisted of a tiny refrigerator and tiny stove, with a tiny table and two chairs stuck in the corner of the room. Thankfully, Reed did take the hint this time, because he spun around and headed in that direction. Only then did Mindy release a breath she'd been unaware of holding, and only then did her world seem to stop spinning out of control.

Still, she could scarcely believe Reed Atchison was there in her apartment. She made a quick survey of their surroundings and wished with all her might that he hadn't come. Everywhere she looked, down to every last detail, her environment fairly shouted *poverty*. From the decades-old furniture to the dingy curtains on the gritty windows, everything looked tired and worn-out and…poor.

Even her Christmas decorations, the ones she'd thought rather cheery until now, seemed cheap and primitive with Reed here. The red-and-green construction-paper chains she'd made, so like the ones she'd put together in elementary school, had seemed kind of charming when she'd strung them above the windows and around the doors two weeks before. And the little plastic tree in the window, even though devoid of lights, had seemed kind of cute when she'd decorated it with little, dime-store candy canes. And the solitary, red-and-white striped stocking—a man's sock from the local thrift store—that was affixed to her radiator now looked ridiculous instead of quaint.

Reed seemed to think so, too, as he took in the decorations, but he said nothing to make his feelings known. Doubtless, he had a huge blue spruce all decked out in silver and gold at his place, she thought. With color-coordinated ornaments hung just so and little white lights that flashed in perfect accord to whatever Christmas music played on the stereo. Her own attempt at capturing the Yuletide spirit must seem pretty pathetic by comparison. Still, it was the best she could do on her salary. And it was in keeping with the rest of the neighborhood's attempt to be as festive as possible.

Because even though the area where Mindy lived might be poor, it was also safe, clean and carried a strong bond of community, she reminded herself. Her neighbors were, by and large, good people. They were just good people who didn't have very much money. There was no shame in living the way she did. She was doing the best she could. And she was a darn sight better off than a lot of folks were.

Nevertheless, for some reason she didn't want Reed to see the extent of her hand-to-mouth existence. Although she knew he was aware of her situation, having him see evidence of how she lived made her feel…

What? she asked herself.

Less than him, she immediately answered. She felt as if she was less of a person than Reed Atchison was. He had everything—money, education, sophistication, social prominence. And she had none of those things. She was a diner waitress, for heaven's sake, one who'd barely managed to finish high school. She'd grown up blue collar, the daughter of a couple of nobodies—one of whom she'd never even met, the other of whom was no longer living. She'd been married to a man of similar background to herself, one who'd left her with even less than the meager possessions she'd had before she married him.

So, really, Mindy supposed, the reason she *felt* as if she was less than Reed Atchison was because she *was* less than Reed Atchison. And she didn't like feeling—or being—that way at all.

The rattle of paper thankfully interrupted her ruminations, and she looked over to see him pulling cartons and foam containers—lots of them—out of one of the sacks. Good Lord, she thought as the parade of food began to seem limitless, it looked as if he'd come ready to feed a party of twelve.

"I got a little bit of everything," he said without turning around, seeming to read her thoughts again in that jarring way he had. "I wasn't sure what you liked. There's even a couple of vegetarian dishes, just in case you don't eat meat. Though, as a pregnant woman, you need to be upping your protein intake by a good thirty or forty grams a day."

"I don't mind meat," she said. "And I've been drinking a lot more milk than I used to. Evie comps us one meal per shift, and I try to make sure I get something substantial." *Even if I rarely eat very much of it.* There was no reason Reed had to know that.

She thought he muttered something in approval but she wasn't sure.

"Iron, too," he said. "You need extra iron. Folic acid is also essential."

"I've been taking prenatal vitamins," she told him. "I'm getting all that."

"Yes, well, vitamins are all well and good, of course," he said as turned his attention to the second sack. "But it doesn't replace good nutrition. You need to eat, so you'll gain some weight. You're far too skinny."

Coming from any other man, Mindy would have wanted to pop him in the eye for saying such a thing. But he was a doctor, confronted by a woman whose pregnancy pretty much amounted to a medical condition. And he was doubtless just offering her his medical opinion, forming a diagnosis based on his professional analysis of her situation in his capacity of physician.

No way was there anything personal in the comment, she told herself. No way could he possibly care about her health in any way other than his doctoral one. Hey, he himself had claimed to believe that people didn't give a fig for each other, right? Why else would he feel that way, unless he was speaking from experience? His concern for her was as a medical professional and nothing more.

Probably.

"Thank you, Doctor," Mindy said. "I'll take it under advisement. Do send me a bill for this visit, will you?"

He halted his actions, his back going rigid at her remark. But he said nothing in response. He just went back to unpacking cartons and containers, lining them up on her minuscule countertop like a portable buffet.

"If you're not hungry," he said, "then I suggest you start with the wonton or egg drop soup. That might stimulate your appetite, and then you can try something a little more ambitious. I can tell you from personal experience that the beef lo mein is terrific."

She took a few experimental steps forward, pausing near the table to lean a hip indolently against it. She hoped she looked casual and carefree, but those were actually the last things she felt at the moment. She watched as he searched her cabinets—all three of them—withdrew two plates and two glasses, then rifled through her two drawers for silverware. With deft efficiency, he set the table for two, pouring her a glass of milk, a half-gallon carton of which he'd also withdrawn from one of the sacks, and filling his glass with a beer that he produced from the other.

When he looked up from his task, her heart kicked up that pittypat-pittypat-pittypat rhythm again, because the smile he wore was anything but professional, anything but medical, anything but doctoral. Before she had a chance to contemplate exactly what that anything *was*, however, the two lamps she'd lit earlier flickered out and the refrigerator, which had been humming along to the conversation quite nicely, suddenly went silent.

"Were you, uh…a little late in paying the electric bill, too?" Reed asked. She could hear the chuckle in his voice, even though the darkness shadowed his expression.

Mindy was grateful for that darkness nonetheless, because she didn't want him to see what was undoubtedly a telltale blush of red that crept into her cheeks at his question. Even though the answer was no, that her utilities were included in her rent, she knew that had they not been, then, more than likely, the sudden lack of electricity probably would have happened anyway, and for precisely the reason he had quoted.

"It's just an old building with old wiring," she said by way of an explanation. "The power goes out a couple of times a month. *Not* because I didn't pay my bills," she hastened to add. "My utilities are included with the rent, which I've always paid on time. Pretty much," she felt compelled to add, being such an honest person.

Which was why it was always so darn cold in the apartment, she muttered to herself. Ed Cranky kept the thermostat set just above the Arctic Tundra setting. Right around the Siberian Gulag setting.

"So, then…you got any candles?" he asked.

Pittypat-pittypat-pittypat went her heart. Oh dear…

"Uh, yeah, I do, actually," she told him. "On top of the fridge, if you can find it."

Reed felt blindly for the big appliance as he waited for his eyes to adjust to the darkness, then, when he located it, felt around the top until his fingers brushed over some stubby candles and a box of wooden matches. Hastily, he scratched a match alongside the box, then lit one candle and snatched up another. As he placed both on a plate at the center of her table, he tried to avoid looking at Mindy.

Just what they needed, he thought wryly. Romantic candlelight for their dinner. Then again, when he recalled the drab surroundings of her apartment, he realized the only thing that would improve this place was dim—very dim—lighting.

He couldn't believe this was where she lived her life outside the diner. Certainly it was clean and tidy enough, but the bare wood floor sported only one thin rug, the curtains were threadbare and the furniture was downright ugly. He remembered Mindy saying her apartment had come furnished and he could readily believe it. No one would *choose* these kinds of furnishings, nor set them up amid such dark, homely, cold surroundings. Especially someone like her, who belonged amid beauty, light and warmth.

And now she was going to lose this meager place, too, however inappropriate it was. Man, life was capricious sometimes.

He added a third squat candle to the other two, and together they would provide enough illumination to enable them to eat their dinner. When he glanced up at Mindy, her face was a pale glowing oval against the darkness, the blond curls that circled her face looking like wisps of a halo. She *was* kind of angelic, he thought. Kind, decent, pretty in a way he could only describe as ethereal. And she loved Christmas.

He nodded toward the feast he had spread on the counter. "Dig in," he told her.

But she was clearly hesitant to do so. "I'm really not very hungry," she said.

"You need to eat," he told her in his best Dr. Kildare voice. "Even if you're not hungry, you should try to put something in your stomach."

She opened her mouth, clearly wanting to object again, then seemed to realize it was pointless. Because it *was* pointless, Reed thought. He wasn't leaving here until she'd eaten a decent meal and promised to stay off her feet. And although she might not know it now, he intended to follow this exact same drill tomorrow night, and the night after. He'd promised her he'd check up on her to make sure she was taking it easy, and by God, Reed Atchison always kept his word.

"Well, maybe I could handle a little soup," she said. "Seeing as how you're going to be such a kitchen Nazi about it."

He smiled. "Vee haf vays of makink you eat," he said in what he knew was a very bad German accent, deciding it would probably be best not to dwell upon how he'd been overcome by such whimsy. "You vill clean your plate, *fräu-

lein, and you vill enjoy every bite. *And* you vill smile vile you are doink it.''

She laughed, and a bubble of warmth exploded in Reed's stomach, warming his entire body before overtaking his heart. She had the most wonderful laugh. Odd, that a woman who'd had the kind of life she had would have such musical laughter. Stranger still was how often—and how naturally—that laughter came.

''Fine,'' she said as she took her seat at the table. ''I'll clean my plate. I'll even smile while I'm doing it. But I'm *not* going to enjoy every bite. I don't care what kind of fascist tactics you use.''

Five

"**W**ow, that was really good."

Reed chuckled at Mindy's total about-face as he helped her stow the last of the leftovers in her refrigerator. She'd eaten enough tonight to feed three pregnant women, he thought with a smile, feeling triumphant for no reason he could name. She really had cleaned her plate—several times, in fact—really had enjoyed every bite, really had smiled while she was doing it. Better than that, though, she'd talked. A lot. As had Reed. Frankly, he couldn't remember the last time he'd enjoyed a meal as much as he had this one.

It was amazing how much they'd shared beyond a simple meal. Mindy was a chatty individual, no doubt about that, and she'd spoken quite freely of her childhood and teenage years.

Reed now knew that she was, like him, an only child and had, like him, lost both of her parents, though one of her losses had come from abandonment instead of death. She'd grown up in South Jersey, just across the river from where he'd grown up himself, and had spent an occasional summer weekend at the Jersey shore—just as he had. Her musical and reading tastes were eclectic—just like his were—and she'd often thought that she might someday like to learn to play the piano. With Reed, it was the saxophone, but the desires were both the same. And on top of all that, they'd both liked the kung pao chicken best.

It was truly phenomenal, he thought now, what you could learn about a person in only one meal. And not just about your dining companion, either, he reflected further.

Although the power was still out, she'd assured him it would be back on before midnight—it always was, she'd said. It was probably just his imagination—or perhaps the faint light of the now sputtering candles—but already she was looking healthier than she had when he'd first met her at the diner. Her cheeks were pink, her eyes bright. Her hair looked soft and shimmery, dancing atop her head in a riot of curls that were just begging for a man's fingers to free them, so he could bury his hands in the silky tresses.

Stop it, he told himself, shoving the strange sensation aside. *You do not want to go there.*

The last thing he needed was to get involved with Mindy Harmon—in anything other than a patron saint capacity, at any rate. He was fulfilling the terms of his bargain with Seth, he reminded himself. Doing a few good deeds for a woman in need. That was it. As soon as he saw Mindy settled somewhere, he'd be on his merry way. Theirs was a friendly relationship, nothing more. And even at that, it was only temporary.

Mindy needed someone in her life who was more stable and caring than Reed could ever hope to be. She needed a man who would cherish her and her baby, a man who would welcome them into his own life and make them a vital part of it. A man who could show his affection for them as easily as Mindy seemed capable of showing how much she cared for others. And that man simply was not Reed Atchison.

Sure, he could keep an eye on her until further notice and he could see to it that she found a place to live. Hell, he'd even hang around until the baby was born, if she'd let him, long enough to make sure she had everything she needed. But after that, he was outta there. Good deed completed, wager fulfilled, no harm done.

He settled the last container on the top shelf of the refrigerator and closed the door, then turned to find Mindy peeking into one of the sacks from the restaurant.

"What? No dessert?" she asked. "Boy, are you a cheap date."

"Hey," he objected. "I've been called many things in my life but never a cheap date."

She rolled her eyes. "Oh, please. You come over to my place with takeout, you don't bring me flowers or candy, not even a bottle of nonalcoholic wine. And now you tell me there's no dessert? How on earth could you think I'd be impressed?"

There was a teasing quality to her voice that made a funny little humming kick up in his chest, made a strange little buzzing erupt in his head. He couldn't recall a woman ever teasing him. All the relationships he'd had with women had been founded on mutual respect and admiration, not playful fun. Whenever he'd asked a woman out—or whenever he'd accepted an invitation from a woman—it had been because he felt as if they had something in common: a stalwart disposition, an appreciation for intelligent conversation, a desire to experience the finer things life had to offer, like elegant dining, enervating theater, intelligent films.

In other words, pretty formal, boring stuff, come to think of it now.

With Mindy, though, he had nothing in common—well, except for all those things they'd discovered over dinner. But he'd be damned if he wasn't having fun. And he was amazed to discover he'd never really had fun with a woman before. More amazing than that, however, was how much he discovered he liked it.

"You want dessert?" he asked, striving for a teasing tone of voice, certain he didn't even come close. How could he, when he'd never teased anyone in his life? "I'll give you dessert," he added. He strode over to where he'd shed his bomber jacket earlier, having tossed it onto the sofa. As the clerk at the Chinese restaurant had totaled his order, Reed had reached into a big fishbowl on the counter and extracted a handful of fortune cookies. He didn't know why. He didn't even like fortune cookies. But something had just made him do it.

Now he tossed one to Mindy. "There," he told her. "There's your dessert. Enjoy."

She caught it easily in both hands, chuckling as she did so. Immediately, she tore off the plastic wrap and snapped the cookie open, then withdrew a long strand of white paper. But her smile fell some as she read it.

"What?" Reed asked, crossing back to the table. "What does it say?"

But she was already rolling it up when he got there and she threw it into one of the sacks that still stood on the counter. "Nothing," she said, nibbling one half of the cookie.

"It had to say something," he objected. "Otherwise, I'm going to demand my twenty-five cents back."

"There you go again, trying to impress me," she said. But somehow, her smile this time didn't quite seem genuine. "Twenty-five whole cents for dessert. You must have been saving your allowance for weeks."

"C'mon," he cajoled, ignoring her obviously forced levity. "What did it say?"

"Nothing," she insisted. "It was one of those generic fortunes that could mean anything."

Reed growled under his breath and snatched the sack from the countertop, thrusting his hand inside.

"Hey!" she cried. "What do you think you're doing?"

"I'm reading your fortune," he said as his fingers closed over the tiny coil of paper.

"But—"

This was ridiculous, he knew. Why he was making such a big deal over something like a fortune cookie was beyond him, but for some reason, it was vitally important that he find out what fate had in store for Mindy Harmon. So before she could halt him—and without acknowledging the fact that her reaction was as strange as his was—he unwound the paper, holding it toward the candles so that he could see the words printed there.

In a last ditch effort to stop him, she curled her fingers around his bare wrist. "Reed..." she said.

He liked the way her voice wrapped itself around his name, marveled at how hearing her say it made everything suddenly seem right. His gaze met hers in the soft candlelight, and his skin seemed to come alive where she had circled his wrist with her fingers. His pulse pounded wildly, and he knew that she felt it, too, beneath her thumb, because her eyes widened in surprise. But she didn't let go of him, and for that he was grateful.

"I just want to see what it says," he told her, all amusement having fled from his voice.

"It's nothing," she insisted halfheartedly.

But he couldn't help himself. As much as he hated to look away from her lovely face, he dropped his gaze to the strand of paper in his hand to see what it said.

The gift of a stranger is much more than it seems.

Well, Reed thought. How oddly...appropriate. That sort of put things into a new perspective, didn't it?

"See?" she said softly. "I told you it didn't mean anything. It makes no sense at all."

Right, he thought. And every cloud had a silver lining, too.

"Boy, who comes up with these things, huh?" he asked. He told himself he only imagined the shakiness in his voice when he spoke. "You're right," he added as he wadded the little piece of paper up again and tossed it back into the sack. "That could mean just about anything."

He wasn't sure, but she seemed to gaze at that paper sack

with a wistful longing. But how could that be? What could that sack possibly hold that she could be longing for, and wistfully at that? Before he could puzzle over its meaning, however, she turned her attention back to him.

"Thanks," she said, her voice softer than it had been, all the teasing gone. "For dinner, I mean. It was awfully nice of you. I haven't eaten that much in one sitting for months."

"You need to eat that much every night," he told her, striving again for cool, detached Dr. Kildare, but sounding way too much like a concerned lover instead.

"Yeah, well, there are enough leftovers in the fridge to feed me for a week, so that shouldn't be a problem," she said with a smile.

"Not this week anyway," he replied. "But what about next week? And the week after that? And the week after that? And just where will you be eating after this week, anyway?"

Her smile fell. "What do you mean?"

"I mean, Mindy, how are you planning to take care of yourself between now and the baby's birth? In one week, the leftovers will be gone, and in just a few days longer than that your landlord will be throwing you out of here. And what will you do when that happens?"

She sighed impatiently. "Look, I told you it's none of your concern."

"It is my concern, dammit," he said, surprised by the vehemence he heard in his own voice. "I care about what happens to you."

"Why?"

"Because—"

He stopped abruptly, not sure he even knew what he had meant to say. He really didn't know why he cared so much about her. He just did. She was a sweet person. She had a good heart. She didn't deserve the crummy lot in life that she'd been given. And if it was within his power to help her— and it *was* within his power to help her—then he wanted to lend a hand.

"You're a nice person," he said, speaking his thoughts

aloud. "You've helped other people, and right now you could use some help yourself. I'm in a position to offer it. That's why."

"But it's not necessary," she said.

"Just let me do it. Let me give you a hand for a few months. Until you're steady on your feet again."

"But why?" she demanded, more forcefully this time. "You don't have to do anything for me."

"Yes, I do."

"*Why?*"

"Because..." He sighed fitfully, extending his hand forward as if trying to pull a reason out of thin air. But all he could come up with was, "Because it's Christmas." Okay, so it was a lame reason. He was hoping it was one she'd go for, seeing as how she was so into the holiday.

But she only gazed at him blankly for a moment. Then, very slowly, she nodded, as if she suddenly understood something that made her very sad. And in a flat voice that only reinforced that impression, she said, "And I'm a convenient Christmas charity for you, right?"

A surge of heat flashed in his belly when he understood what she meant. She thought he was only here because he felt sorry for her, when in fact, just the opposite was true. He'd come here tonight because he was feeling sorry for himself. And he was only now realizing that.

Immediately, he shook his head at her assumption. "No, that's not it at all."

"Isn't it?"

"No, Mindy, it's—"

"You're only doing this to fulfill the terms of a bet," she interrupted. "Because you feel obligated. Because this time of year brings out the good Samaritan in people."

"No, that's not—"

"You look at me and you see some pathetic, needy woman who can't take care of herself, let alone her unborn child, and you think you can do a better job of it yourself."

"No, I—"

"And, hey, you'll feel a lot better about yourself and your own life after you've seen the way I struggle to survive. You'll be able to go home at night and lie in bed and think, 'Maybe my life isn't perfect, but thank God I've got it better than Mindy Harmon.'"

Her voice broke a little as she finished the sentence, and she clamped her mouth shut tight. But he was fairly certain there had been plenty more she wanted to say. Where before she had been all soft and mellow, suddenly she seemed like a towering Amazon—all five feet two inches of her. And suddenly, Reed, God help him, saw her as considerably more than a pregnant woman who needed a helping hand. He saw her as a woman. Period. Beautiful. Vivacious. Desirable.

"Oh, I'll almost certainly lie in bed thinking about you at night, Mindy," he said before he could stop himself, his voice coming out rough, rusty and reluctant. "But I promise you won't be pathetic and needy in those thoughts. Well, maybe needy. But not in the way you think."

He couldn't imagine what had made him voice such thoughts out loud—they'd just exploded in his brain and erupted from his mouth before he could stop them. But once uttered, there was no way he could take them back. And strangely, once uttered, he wasn't sure he wanted to take them back. He had no idea why.

Mindy, however, looked as if she really wished he could, really wished he would. In fact, she looked as if she were going to cry. Then, much to Reed's horror, she did.

It wasn't a burst of outraged emotion, just a single, fat tear that tumbled down her cheek. But then she blinked, and another joined it. Then another and another and another, slow, tiny rivulets of water that followed each other one by one down her face.

"Mindy..." he began.

But instead of finishing whatever he had been about to say—which was good because, frankly, he wasn't sure what he *had* been about to say—he closed what little distance separated them, until his body was nearly flush with hers. Barely a hairbreadth of air separated them, and he fancied he could feel her heat mingling with his own.

His instincts told him to reach out to her. His reason told him that to do so would be a very big mistake. For all of one second he considered his options, then he lifted his hands and cupped them lightly over her shoulders.

"What is it?" he asked. "What's wrong?"

His words seemed to break a spell of some kind, because only then did she seem to realize what was happening. Her eyes widened in surprise—or perhaps terror, it was hard for him to say—and she quickly jerked away from him.

"Mindy…" he repeated.

She shook her head slowly, silently. Then she took a few hasty steps in retreat until she hit the kitchen counter with her fanny, something that rather impeded her progress.

Once again, Reed surrendered to his instincts, which commanded him to go to her and try again. But this time when he approached her, he did it much more carefully, much more cautiously. And this time, when he extended his hands toward her, she only flinched a little before allowing him to touch her. But the moment he settled his hands gently over her shoulders, she began to cry again.

"What's wrong? Why are you crying?" he asked, striving for a gentleness he wasn't quite feeling. The sight of her tears, of her despondency, was making him crazy. A moment ago, she'd been laughing and vital and warm. Now, suddenly, she looked hopeless and helpless. And he couldn't help but feel as if he'd been responsible somehow for the change in her. He just wished he could figure out what, exactly, he'd done wrong.

"What did I do?" he asked, putting voice to his troubled thoughts. "What, Mindy?"

In response, she only closed her eyes, something that squeezed even more tears down along her cheeks. Then, very softly, she said, "You made me…"

"What?" he said. "Tell me. Whatever it was, whatever it is, I'll stop. I promise."

"No," she replied softly, her voice a scant whisper. "Don't stop, please."

"Fine, I won't stop," he growled, his frustration compounding. "Just tell me what I did."

She opened her eyes then, and he didn't think he'd ever seen that shade of green anywhere before. The tears gave depth to her sorrow, clarity to her fear. And something inside him that had been knotted tight for decades slowly began to unfurl.

"What did I do?" he repeated, curling his fingers more insistently into her shoulders.

"You made me feel..." she began.

"What?"

"You made me feel something that I haven't felt for a very long time," she finally finished. "And then you touched me like...like..." She swallowed with some difficulty, but never finished the statement. She only said, "Nobody's touched me like...like that...not for a very long time. Maybe not ever."

"Oh, Mindy..."

He couldn't help what he did next. He really couldn't. It just sort of...happened. One minute, she was gazing up at him with those green, green eyes and the next, he was lowering his head to hers. He didn't know why. He just wanted to get closer to her for some reason. Wanted to get closer to her and...something else, too...something more...

Even with his eyes closed, he found her mouth with no trouble at all. Maybe because she helped him a little bit by meeting him halfway. Or maybe because, for once in his life, he knew exactly what he wanted. In any case, he framed her face gently in his hands, then brushed her lips gently with his own, once, twice, three times. He hesitated before he did anything else, wanting to savor that small gesture, just in case it never happened again. Then, reluctantly, he pulled back to gaze upon her face, no longer certain for sure that she was even real.

But she was real. He knew that immediately. He could feel her heat, could smell the clean, soapy scent of her skin, could hear her rapid breathing, could see the way her pupils had expanded with her desire. And if he wanted, he knew he could find out what she tasted like, too.

He wanted. Most definitely. So he dipped his head toward hers again and covered her mouth more completely this time, more possessively, more masterfully. And once again, Mindy met him halfway, tentatively, curiously, needfully. Reed, naturally, was only too willing to fulfill that need. And as he satisfied her, he could take a little for himself, too. Then he reminded himself that it was Christmastime. Better to give than to receive, right?

Unable to help himself, he traced her bottom lip with the tip of his tongue and at her slight gasp of surprise he slipped inside her mouth. She tasted wonderful, like…good fortune, he thought, surprised at his whimsy. And then he ceased to think at all, because a rumble of need shook him, commanding that he taste her more deeply still.

She groaned at such a thorough invasion but didn't push him away. On the contrary, she gripped the fabric of his sweater in both fists, curling her fingers tightly into the woven knit, pulling him closer, mindless of the fact that he was already as close as he could be. Reed threaded his fingers through the loose curls at her nape, then shoved one hand higher, to the knot of fabric holding her ponytail in place. With one quick, effortless gesture, he removed it and felt the tumble of silk fall down over his hands.

Immediately, he buried his fingers in the rioting tresses, cupping one hand at the base of her skull, tipping her head back so that he could drag openmouthed kisses along her jaw and her throat. The fists she had closed against his chest loosened then, her fingers splaying open across his chest, scooting up to his shoulders, closing tight once more. He dropped one hand to the small of her back, pushing her body into his, groaning himself at the feel of her in his hands, along his torso.

She was so soft, so warm, so very tempting. And it had been so long since he'd held a woman this way, so long since there had been any meaning in holding a woman this way.

And then he wondered if there had ever been any meaning in holding a woman at all, until now.

He nosed the neckline of her sweatshirt aside and nuzzled the tender flesh at the base of her throat, taunting her with the tip of his tongue before tasting her more fully. A fire had ignited in his belly at some point and now it blazed steadily inside him, simmering his blood, sparking his need, torching whatever vague sense of reason he had left. And still Mindy clung to him, still she demanded more. And still Reed needed more. So much more.

He loosed the hair he gripped in his hand and skimmed his fingers lower, down along the back of her neck, around to the front, along one elegant collarbone. Then he reversed his hand to brush the backs of his fingers slowly, oh so slowly, down over her breast. She gasped again at the contact, but Reed returned his mouth to hers, swallowing her objection whole as he rotated his hand again to cup her fully in his palm.

"Oh," she murmured. "Oh, please..."

He wasn't sure what she was asking him to do, whether she wanted him to stop or go, speed up or slow down. So he hesitated for a moment, waiting to see what she would do. Almost imperceptibly, Mindy squeezed his upper arm, as if uttering a silent request. Reed pulled back far enough to look into her face, and what he saw there nearly stopped his heart.

She looked as if he'd betrayed her. Her eyes were filled with an unmistakable sadness and pain, and he couldn't for the life of him figure out why. He had thought she wanted this, too. She had responded so eagerly, so needfully, so enthusiastically. He had thought she felt the same way he did. He had thought she wanted him, too.

Obviously, he'd been wrong. Obviously, she didn't want him at all.

Immediately, he released her, taking a giant step backward to show her that he had no intention of taking advantage of her. For a moment, she didn't move. She stood stock-still, staring at him, her fingers still curled loosely together, clutching nothing now but air. Her eyes... God, her eyes. They were so deep, so green, so full of sadness. And he was the one who had caused that. If only he could figure out why.

"Mindy, I'm sorry," he said quickly. "I didn't mean for that to happen. Especially after I promised you I wouldn't... I'm sorry," he finished hastily.

Instead of making her feel better, his words only seemed to compound her melancholy. "No," she said softly, "I'm sure you didn't mean for it to happen. And I'm sure you're sorry it did."

"I just... I mean, it's just... I didn't... What I wanted was... I mean, I *didn't* want..."

He gave up trying to explain when he realized he had no explanation to give her. Well, none that she'd find acceptable, anyway. None that she would understand. He'd wanted her, that was all. He'd wanted her closeness, her warmth, her vitality. But he should have waited until she'd offered it to him, he told himself now. He shouldn't have just reached out to take it.

"I... That won't happen again," he assured her. Funny, though, how he felt in no way assured of that himself. "I promise you, Mindy, it won't."

She nodded. "I know it won't. Because you'll be leaving right now. And you won't be coming back. Ever. Not to my apartment. Not to the diner. Consider your good deed done, your wager fulfilled. There's no reason why we'll ever have to see each other again. Okay?"

He didn't answer her. He couldn't. There was no way he'd agree to something like that.

At his silence, she wrapped her arms around herself, as if she suddenly felt cold. "Okay?" she demanded, more forcefully this time.

Still, Reed said nothing.

And Mindy only stared.

Clearly, this was not a good time to try to figure out what the hell was going on. Reed's emotions were raw, his thoughts a complete jumble. And Mindy was obviously suffering from the same thing. So without a further word, he strode toward the couch to retrieve his bomber jacket. Silently, he shrugged into it and silently, he made his way to the front door.

He had intended to leave that way, without comment, because he just didn't know what to say. But as he pulled the door open, he realized that to do so would only make things worse. So he spun back around, only to find that Mindy hadn't altered her pose at all.

She still stood with her arms crossed over her midsection, a frail splash of color in the fading candlelight. Her hair tumbled down around her face, giving the impression of a halo again, but she was much too small and pale and fragile—and human—to be an angel.

"I'll see you," he said, thinking that was the only thing he could say that would be even remotely honest.

She shook her head. "No, you won't."

"This isn't over, Mindy," he said, more forcefully this time. "Not by a long shot. There's too much here to just let it go."

"There's nothing here," she countered. "What happened just now...it was just..."

"What?"

But she only shook her head silently again.

"I'll see you," he repeated.

And before she could deny it, he stepped through the door and closed it softly behind himself.

Six

Reed was as good as his word. Mindy discovered that the very next evening, when he knocked on her front door again, armed with two brown paper sacks, again, looking luscious and tempting in his faded jeans and bulky sweater and bomber jacket—again. The only thing different this time was that the sweater was heather-gray and the paper sacks held Italian— she knew that by the aroma of garlic and pesto that replaced the previous evening's soy and teriyaki.

Oh, and another thing that was different was that he looked infinitely more uncomfortable than he had the last time he had darkened her door. Last night he had appeared confident, knowing and unflappable, as if he didn't for one moment doubt his behavior or question his intentions. Tonight, however, he appeared to be uncertain, confused and very flappable indeed. Which was just as well, she supposed. Because that was exactly how she was feeling herself.

"Don't slam the door in my face," he said by way of a greeting.

She tamped down the smile that threatened, along with the wave of warmth that accompanied it. "Gosh, you even read minds," she replied mildly. "Is there no end to your super-human abilities?"

He eyed her with much bemusement. "What are you talking about?"

She shrugged, hoping the gesture came off as nonchalant, when in fact she felt very, uh…"chalant"…indeed. "Well, gee, you're a cardiologist, aren't you?" she pointed out un-necessarily. "A surgeon who saves lives, which in itself puts you on the right hand of God, doesn't it? But that's not enough for you, is it, saving lives in the hospital? You have to go after perfectly healthy people you don't think can take care of themselves and try to save their lives, too."

He frowned at her. "For one thing, although I agree that some of my colleagues do in fact suffer from the God complex you describe, I'm not one of them. Believe me—I'm fully aware of my humanity. More so lately than I ever have been before."

She told herself not to think too much about his cryptic remark, which was just as well, because he evidently had a lot more that he wanted to say.

"For another thing," he continued, "I wouldn't exactly say you're perfectly healthy. You nearly passed out at the diner the other day, you've suffered a pretty bad burn and your pregnancy looks like it's exhausting you."

"Oh, now just hold on one—"

"And for another thing," he interrupted her, "I wouldn't exactly say you can take care of yourself, because in a matter of days, you—and your unborn child—will be on the streets in the dead of winter, with no place to call home."

"Hey, that's not my—"

"And for *another* thing," he went on relentlessly, ignoring her objections. But he halted before completing the thought, snapped his mouth shut tight and never completed whatever he had intended to say.

Mindy eyed him curiously. "What?" she asked, wondering

why she did so, when she had just been arguing to the contrary everything he'd said. Or, rather, had *tried* to argue to the contrary. He'd sort of prevented her from succeeding at that.

"For another thing," he said again, more softly this time. But again, he hesitated. Finally, he shrugged once, quickly, and said, "Maybe I'm not doing this to save your life, Mindy."

Now she really eyed him curiously. "No?"

He shook his head. "No. Maybe I'm doing it to save my own."

Her confusion compounded at his bewildering statement. "What do you mean?"

But instead of answering her question, he asked one of his own. "Can I come in? I promise I'll behave myself tonight."

Which was all well and good for *him*, Mindy thought. *His* behavior wasn't what worried her. She was far more concerned about her own. She still wasn't sure what had happened the night before, why the two of them had ended up in each other's arms the way they had. She simply hadn't been able to resist him. He was so handsome and he'd been so kind, and they'd shared such warm, comfortable conversation over dinner. She'd forgotten how much she enjoyed simply having the company of another human being. She hadn't realized how lonely she'd become over the last several months. Or how lonely she had been in her marriage, for that matter. It had just been so pleasant to have him there, in any capacity, to keep the solitude at bay.

But in allowing herself to feel those things, she'd unwittingly let down her guard. She had forgotten that the two of them had nothing in common, had forgotten that they were worlds apart, had forgotten that she had no business wanting him. She'd forgotten that he wasn't for her and never would be. She'd forgotten that, to him, she was little more than a Christmas charity.

And then, when he'd said what he had about thinking of her while he was in bed, about her being needy, but not the way she meant... Mindy closed her eyes for a moment as the same heated, desperate feelings that had washed over her the night before threatened to engulf her again. He'd made her feel like a woman—a desirable woman. And it had been a very long time since she had felt like that. In some ways, she wondered if she had *ever* felt quite the way he'd made her feel the night before.

Her husband hadn't been the most attentive lover in the world. Sam had been greedy and demanding when it came to sex, had cared more for his own needs than he had for hers. There had been so many times when they'd made love that she had been left feeling unsatisfied, unfulfilled and terribly empty inside. Times when he had, quite literally, rolled over and fallen asleep, before she'd even come close to achieving climax herself.

Somehow, she suspected that Reed wouldn't be like that at all. She sensed that he would take care with a woman, would see to his lover's needs before seeing to his own. And with that solitary comment he'd uttered last night, he had made her want him, desperately. And human being that she was, she had responded to that wanting, had fallen into that kiss as if it might be the last she ever received.

It made no sense. Really, she scarcely knew him. That hadn't stopped her from wanting him, though. Or from needing him. She only wished she could have him. But that would never—could never—be.

"Mindy?"

His voice rippled over her like a warm rush of wind, and she opened her eyes. Only then did she realize how immersed in her fantasy she had become. But the sight of him standing there at her front door did nothing to dispel the lingering desires that flamed in her belly and licked at her soul. Instead, she realized, much to her dismay, seeing him again only made her want him that much more.

Although she knew it would be foolish to invite him inside, she stepped out of the way and gestured him in. And as he strode past her, she inhaled deeply that singular scent she would always associate with him. It was the aroma of clean, healthy male, of utter and complete masculinity. And it thrust her awareness of him up to the next—and more dangerous—level.

"I already have leftovers to last me a couple of weeks," she reminded him as she closed the door softly behind herself and leaned back against it. "What am I supposed to do with all this?"

He shrugged. "Freeze it." He met her gaze levelly as he added, very meaningfully, she thought, "Oops. I forgot. In a couple of weeks, you'll be on the streets. You won't have a freezer. How thoughtless of me." He hesitated a telling beat before adding, "Then again, I guess you'll have all of the entire outdoors to act as your freezer, won't you? So this shouldn't pose a problem to you at all."

"Very funny," she muttered, crossing her arms over her midsection, already feeling the chill.

"I wish it was funny," he said. "But it's pretty much the truth, isn't it? You still haven't found a new place to live, have you?"

She shook her head. "But I'll find something."

"You've already found something," he told her. "My condo in Cherry Hill. It's yours for the taking."

"No, thank you," she said through gritted teeth.

"Why not?" he demanded. "I'm not using it. It's just sitting there empty. There's no reason why you shouldn't stay there until you find another place of your own."

"There's a very good reason," she countered.

"Well, I wish to hell you'd tell me what it is."

She glared at him. "It's…because."

"Because?" he echoed dubiously.

She nodded. "Because."

"Because why?"

"Just because, dammit. Leave it alone."

This time Reed was the one to glare. His grip on the two paper sacks grew tighter. "No," he said in a low, level voice.

Even though she'd heard him perfectly well, Mindy asked, "What did you say?"

"I said no. I won't leave it alone. And I won't leave *you* alone."

"Reed, I'm not your responsibility."

"You *are* my responsibility."

She pushed herself away from the door, and, her arms still wrapped tightly around her midsection, took a few steps forward. "And just how do you figure that?" she demanded.

"You're a human being," he said, his own voice none too benevolent. "We're from the same species. We need to look out for each other."

She eyed him curiously. "You learned that in biology, I guess, huh?"

"Actually, it was in humanities."

She nodded, sighing with put-upon patience. "I should have guessed. You're a transcendental surgeon, is that it?"

He smiled, the first genuine smile she'd seen from him since last night, and something inside her that had been frozen solid began to grow warm and fluid. "Just call me Dr. Gandhi," he said.

She couldn't fight the smile that curled her lips in response to his. "And here I thought you were Dr. Grinch."

He chuckled. "First I'm Dr. Scrooge, then Dr. Grinch. What next?"

"Now you seem more like Dr. Jekyll," Mindy told him as she took a few more steps forward, loosening her hold on herself some. "What exactly are you talking about?"

This time he was the one to shake his head. "Just that lately I seem to be a man of many identities and many moods." He turned toward the kitchen and began to make his way in that direction. She wasn't sure, but she thought he added something that sounded like, "And I'm not sure which one is the real me anymore."

She decided not to comment on that. Not just because she didn't think he'd intended for her to hear what he said, but because she wasn't sure she understood what he meant by the remark. So she only watched from the other side of the room while he unpacked the bags as he had the night before and tried to assure herself that tonight would be different, because tonight she'd be on her guard.

Unfortunately, when he turned around to face her, her guard beat a very hasty retreat. Because tonight, he looked even more handsome, even more wonderful, even more desirable, than he had the evening before. And recalling again the kiss that the two of them had shared less than twenty-four hours ago, Mindy felt more needy, more lonely, more hopeful, than she had ever felt in her life.

It was going to be a long night, she thought. She only hoped she fared better this time than she had the evening before.

Just please, whatever happens, don't let the power go out.

She held her breath for a moment, as if the thought that unwound in her head might jinx them and douse the lights. But after one heartbeat, then two, then three, the lights were still on, and the refrigerator still hummed happily in the corner. She battled a wave of déjà vu as Reed pulled out the last of the foam containers, along with a bottle of the same kind of beer he'd had the night before and a small carton of milk for Mindy.

"I hope you like fettucine Alfredo," he said. "It was about the fattiest, most high-calorie thing on the menu. I figured you could use it. And there's spumoni ice cream for dessert."

He spun around then and threw her a smile that was anything but confident. Somehow, his uncertainty made her feel a whole lot better about what was going on between them. If only she could pin down exactly what it was that *was* going on between them. Still, she was grateful that they had both evidently decided by mutual—and silent—decree that they wouldn't mention their kiss of the night before. No sense rehashing that, after all. It wasn't likely to happen again.

"But you can only have dessert," he added, "if you clean your plate."

Knowing there was little chance he would back down—after all, look how last night had turned out—Mindy sighed and covered what little distance remained between her and the fragrant food. And all the while, she tried to ignore the wave of desire and hunger—which, strangely, had absolutely nothing to do with the food—that very nearly overwhelmed her. Then, with a final shrug that pretty much dispelled—or at least, over-shadowed—whatever doubts lingered, she nodded.

"Fettucine Alfredo sounds wonderful," she said. "And I adore spumoni ice cream."

By the third night, when Reed showed up again—the sweater he wore with his blue jeans was berry-colored on that occasion—with two more paper sacks—those bearing Mexican food—Mindy began to sense a pattern. It held up the next night, in the form of a navy-blue sweater and sacks bearing Thai, and the night after that—green sweater, Greek food.

However, on the fifth night, there was a slight alteration. Reed's blue jeans were replaced by a pair of disreputable-looking painter's pants, and instead of a tidy, tailored sweater he wore a faded, stretched-out sweatshirt bearing the word *Harvard*. Instead of paper sacks, he gripped a large cooler in one hand and had several broken down cardboard boxes tucked under the other arm.

So much for patterns.

Still, Mindy couldn't help but smile at him when she saw him standing there even though, for once, she *had* dressed for the occasion—or, at least, what she had *thought* would be the occasion—in a pair of black leggings and a long, dark-green tunic. She'd even let down her hair and applied a little makeup, though she hesitated to identify her reasons for doing so. She was just tired of feeling frumpy around him, she'd told herself as she'd brushed on a little mascara and applied a light color to her lips. She was tired of seeing how cool and hand-some he always was and how dowdy and casual she had come to feel by comparison.

Now, however, it appeared that she had jumped the gun a bit. Just what, exactly, was he planning for the evening?

"Gosh, and here I was with a hankering for German food tonight," she said, hoping her voice held none of the confusion she felt.

He shrugged. "I figured we could just heat up some of those leftovers before we started packing and cleaning up the place."

She eyed him warily. "Packing? Cleaning?"

"Packing your stuff and cleaning the apartment," he clarified, as if they'd made some prior arrangements to exactly that effect. "Since you rented this place furnished, I figure you can't have more than four or five boxes full of things to take. And since you're obviously such a neatnik, the cleaning shouldn't take long. You'll be able to get your damage deposit back. We ought to be able to knock this whole thing out with pretty little effort. You can be settled in at my place by bedtime."

She gazed at him in silence for a moment, battling the heat that suddenly shook her inside and out. But it wasn't the heat of resentment or insult, which was what she told herself she should be feeling by his presumption. It was the warmth of relief and gratitude that welled up instead.

In spite of her reaction, however, she said softly, "It's not necessary."

In response, he strode forward, clearly assuming that she would move out of his way. And, naturally, he assumed correctly, because the moment he took a step forward, Mindy took a step to the side and he breezed past her without a second's hesitation.

"If memory serves," he said as he went by, "you have less than a week to be out of this place."

"That's right," she told him. "I still have a whole six days to find a place to live." Even to her own ears, the statement sounded pretty lame. Nevertheless, she clung to it as if it were a lifeline.

He turned around and eyed her with what appeared to be indulgence, but still Mindy found it hard to work up any amount of annoyance. Because, deep down, she knew it was futile to object to anything he might say. She knew better than anyone what a lousy immediate future she had. Thoughts of that had, after all, kept her awake the last several nights. Well, thoughts of that, coupled with thoughts of Reed Atchison.

"Even if you find a place by then," he said, "you'll still have to wait a bit before you can move in. There will be paperwork for the new landlord and, if it's a halfway-decent place, they'll want to run a check on you before letting you move in. At best, you're still going to need a place for a few days. At worst, you're going to need a place for a lot longer than that. And I just so happen to have a place. It's pointless for you to keep turning me down."

Mindy knew that. She did. Not a day had passed since he had initially voiced his offer that she hadn't asked herself why she was so reluctant to take him up on it. She couldn't put it down anymore to not knowing him well enough. After the last few nights spent sharing dinner and conversation with him—not to mention a single, soul-shattering kiss, which she wouldn't, of course, mention, because mentioning it just made her feel things that were better left unmentioned—she felt as if she knew him better than just about anyone else of her acquaintance.

She knew, for instance, that his education had come in the form of expensive boarding schools, that he knew how to play polo, enjoyed sailing and never missed a book by Alice Hoffman or a movie that featured Emma Thompson. He had no brothers or sisters, his parents were deceased and he didn't see much of his other sundry and scattered relatives. He had majored in biology as an undergrad, with a minor in philosophy, and had briefly—very briefly—entertained the idea of a career as a teacher. He'd always wanted a boa constrictor when he was a little boy but had been forced to make do with the family spaniels, because his mother had been, if nothing else, a sane woman.

And Mindy knew, too, that he was a nice guy. And he seemed genuinely interested in helping her out, for no other reason than that it was the right thing to do. He had a place where she could stay that was safe, clean and convenient to her work. And she believed him when he assured her he wouldn't take advantage of the arrangement.

But still...

"Mindy?" he asked. "How about it? You can be settled in within a matter of hours."

In spite of her little pep talk with herself, she was still reluctant to go along. Why? She honestly couldn't say. There was just something about accepting his offer that didn't sit well with her. Maybe it was because she knew she'd never be able to pay him back, and the thought of being so indebted to him, for the rest of her life, was daunting, to say the least. Maybe it was because she just wasn't comfortable accepting charity from someone like him.

Or maybe it was just because she was afraid of what would happen if she did. Not because of anything he might do, but because of what she might do herself. At this point, Mindy didn't trust her feelings at all. And she'd never made wise choices when it came to men. Heaven only knew what would happen to her with prolonged exposure to Reed. She might very well lose a part of herself to him, a part she would never get back, a part he would never be able to return. And living without that part, she feared, might just be too difficult for her to manage.

"I've made a few calls over the last couple of days," she said, shoving her concerns aside for the moment.

His expression shifted to one of wariness. "What kind of calls?"

She licked her lips a little anxiously and gazed at a point over his left shoulder. "To a couple of shelters nearby."

"Shelters?" he echoed incredulously.

She nodded but still couldn't quite meet his gaze. "One said it could accommodate me until the middle of January, maybe longer. But by then, I should be able to find something."

"Shelters?" he repeated in the same tone of voice, as if he hadn't even heard what she'd said after that point.

She nodded again, a bit more vigorously. "It's a perfectly

good arrangement," she told him. "And I've been approved for food stamps, too," she added. "So I'll be able to feed myself after I do find a place."

"Food stamps?" Still that note of disbelief clung to his words.

"And then," she continued, pretending she was totally unconcerned about her situation, "once the baby comes, I'll be accepted into the WIC program."

"Welfare?" he exclaimed. "You'd rather go on welfare than accept my offer of a place to stay?"

She jutted up her chin defiantly. "It's not welfare," she told him. "Not exactly. And even if it was, there's nothing wrong with welfare. I've been working since I was sixteen years old, paying taxes that support those programs, and now, when I need them, they're there for me. There's nothing wrong with that," she repeated, more adamantly this time.

She was *not* going to put up with his snobbery. Not when she was doing something that was perfectly within her rights, perfectly acceptable, perfectly honorable.

"I didn't mean it like that," he said.

"Didn't you?"

He expelled a long, weary sigh, then set the cooler down on the floor and laid the boxes on the table. "Look, I know there's nothing wrong with taking advantage of social programs. When you have *nowhere else to go*," he said, emphasizing each word. "But you, Mindy, you have somewhere else to go. You have someone else to rely on. There's no reason to turn to social programs when you have a...a..."

"A what?" she asked when he faltered over the word. "A sponsor? A patron? Why don't we just call it what it really is—a sugar daddy?"

"A *friend*," he corrected her, frowning. "Why won't you let me be your friend?"

She hesitated before answering him aloud, answering herself silently first. Because she didn't want to be his friend, that was why. Because she wanted something more from him than that. Something that she knew she shouldn't want, something that she knew she could never have.

"I just don't want to take advantage of you," she said softly.

He uttered a sound that was somewhere in between a laugh and sob. "Take advantage of *me?*" he said. "Here I thought you were worried that I'd be trying to take advantage of *you.*"

"I don't feel that way anymore," she said quietly. "Now that I've gotten to know you, I realize you'd never..."

"What?" he asked.

She exhaled softly. "I know you'd never do something like that."

"Then why won't you let me do something nice for you?"

She still didn't know how to answer that, so she remained silent.

"Mindy, please," he said, more gently this time. He sighed again and smiled a small, sad smile. "There's no way you'd be taking advantage of me. This is something I want to do for you. And for me. If you'll just let me."

But still she hesitated.

So he took a step forward. Then another. And another. And he kept coming until he stood right before her, with barely a breath of space between them. He lifted a hand toward her face, then hesitated, as if silently requesting permission to touch her. And because she was simply too stunned to move away, she just stood there, staring at him. Clearly taking her lack of response as a positive reply, Reed cupped her jaw gently in his palm, winding a single strand of hair around his thumb when he did.

The touch was so gentle, so innocent, so undemanding, that Mindy felt her eyes flutter closed. Involuntarily, before she could stop herself, she turned her face into his hand. She felt the stroke of his thumb along her cheek once, twice, three times, and then he brought his other hand up to join the first, framing her face tenderly and with great care.

"If you won't do it for me," he said, his voice a quiet caress on her troubled thoughts, "and if you won't do it for yourself, then do it...do it for the baby."

Oooh, low blow, she thought. How was she supposed to turn him down now? Especially when he touched her the way he was touching her, spoke in the voice he was speaking in, made her feel all the things he was making her feel...?

Whoa, all the more reason to turn him down, she thought, opening her eyes as she pulled away gently. There was definitely something between them. She just couldn't quite say what. One thing she did know, though, whatever it was wouldn't last. Not on his part, at any rate. She was a poor, pregnant diner waitress with limited resources and few prospects. He was a wealthy, educated surgeon who existed in a world completely removed from her own. Whatever he felt for her, it was generated by his concern for her welfare, his fear that she couldn't take care of herself, his sense of duty as a human being. And all that had simply come about because of Christmas. He wasn't at all inspired by what motivated her feelings for him. He couldn't be, she told herself.

He just couldn't.

Still, she had more than herself to think about these days, didn't she? A lot more. Instinctively, she moved her hand to her belly and opened it over her burgeoning womb. There was a baby in there, she reminded herself—as if she needed reminding. A baby who demanded warmth and nourishment, and peace and quiet in order to grow strong and healthy. Especially seeing as how, once he or she was born, there would be little enough of any of those things.

Right now, though, Mindy and her baby could have them all. She could give her unborn child exactly the environment necessary to promote a happy, healthy birth. All she had to do was tell Reed that she accepted his offer. All she had to do was put aside her pride—and her fear for her own feelings—for a little while. All she had to do was accept the fact that she needed help right now, and he was someone who could help her.

Why was that so hard for her to manage, when she would

do exactly the same thing for him if their situations were reversed?

She just had to make sure she squelched—or at least, ignored—the strange stirrings of emotion she was beginning to feel for Reed. Certainly she would have to make sure she resisted acting upon it. But she could do that, couldn't she? After all, it was for her baby. A mother learned to make sacrifices early on. She had to stop thinking in terms of herself and look at the big picture. And the big picture included a lot more than just Mindy now.

"All right," she said, taking a step backward lest she be completely overwhelmed by him. "I accept your offer. But only for as long as it takes me to find a new apartment for myself." Slowly, she caressed the soft mound of her belly. "For us," she amended. And then, not quite as an afterthought, she added, "Thank you, Reed. I really do appreciate it."

Seven

"**W**here's your Christmas tree?"

As he deposited on the living room floor the last of three boxes containing all of Mindy Harmon's worldly possessions, Reed went rigid. He tried to tell himself it was because the thermostat in his Cherry Hill condo was set at an energy-saving sixty degrees and *not* because of her question—which he shoved quickly and conveniently aside, so that he could instead berate himself over the fact that he should have stopped by here on his way to her place to turn up the heat. A good time might have been, oh…that very afternoon, when he'd brought in groceries to stock the place. The thing was, even then, he hadn't been sure she'd be coming. And he decided not to ponder his gratitude and relief that she was here now.

Instead, he straightened, trying to come up with a good answer for her question. Thankfully, however, she provided one herself.

"Oh, that's right," she said. "I forgot. You're not living

here right now. Why would you go to all the trouble of putting up a tree?''

Why indeed? Reed wondered. Maybe because…he considered Christmas to be a real pain in the butt? Maybe because…the last thing he wanted to do was celebrate a season of giving, reunion and family? Maybe because…he found the whole idea of comfort and joy, and may your days be merry and bright, and God rest ye merry gentlemen to be a trifle unrealistic in this day and age?

Bah. Humbug.

''Yeah, well, even if I were staying here at the moment,'' he said, ''I seriously doubt that I would have put up a tree.''

The words were out of his mouth before he could stop them, but much to his surprise, Mindy chuckled in response.

''Oh, that's right,'' she said in a teasing voice. ''I forgot that, too. You're Dr. Scrooge, aren't you? Or is it Dr. Grinch today?''

Her smile was bright when he met her gaze, but it quickly dimmed when she noted his expression, which he figured probably mirrored his feelings—which were, in a word, grim.

''You're serious, aren't you?'' she asked, obviously mystified by his response. ''You wouldn't have decorated even if you were living here, would you?''

He shook his head. ''Why bother? I never do anything special for Christmas. In fact, I don't celebrate Christmas at all.''

She nodded, suddenly understanding. ''I'm sorry. I shouldn't have presumed you'd celebrate Christmas. But then…'' she looked around. ''You don't have a menorah, either, so I guess you don't celebrate Hanukkah.''

Another shake of his head. ''No.''

''Why not?''

''I'm not Jewish.''

''Oh. But…''

''And I don't celebrate Kwanzaa or Ramadan, either, if you're interested,'' he told her. Might as well just get it all out in the open.

''You're an atheist?'' she asked.

"No. I just don't celebrate Christmas, that's all."

"But…why not?" she insisted.

He expelled an exasperated sound. He really, really, really didn't want to have this conversation. Not now. Not ever.

"I mean, I know you've gone out of your way to be Mr. Grinchy Ebenezer Scrooge and all that," she continued, "but I honestly didn't think you took it to heart. I just thought you were one of those people who were disenchanted with the whole commercialization of the holiday. I didn't realize it was the holiday itself that made you so…"

"Grinchy?" he finished for her. "Scroogey?"

She nodded.

He inhaled a deep breath and released it slowly, wishing there was some easy, understandable way to explain things to her. But what he finally decided on was a roughly muttered, halfhearted, "It's really none of your business, Mindy."

She set her jaw tight. "Funny, that never stopped you from invading *my* life."

"Touché," he mumbled.

"Look, I just think it's kind of funny that you wouldn't celebrate Christmas, at least in some small way, if you don't have any religious objections."

"Not everybody gets all sappy and maudlin this time of year, all right?" he said, regretting the bitterness that laced his words. "Dammit. Can we please talk about something else?"

"But—"

"Please?"

He could tell she was in no way appeased, but she nodded reluctantly. "Okay."

Relieved, he launched into his care-and-feeding-of-the-condo speech, giving her a quick tour of the premises, pointing out the thermostat and hot water heater, providing her with the rudimentaries where the operation of the garbage disposal and dishwasher were concerned. She listened attentively to all of his instructions, nodding silently as they went, never saying a word. Somehow, though, he knew she was barely listening, that her thoughts were focused somewhere else entirely. And judging by the not-so-veiled interest of her numerous glances his way, Reed was pretty sure he knew where those thoughts were focused.

"Look," he said as he concluded the tour in the kitchen, "Christmas was just never a big deal for me, okay?"

She didn't seem at all surprised by the sudden change of subject. "Your family didn't celebrate it when you were a kid?" she asked.

"Oh, they celebrated, all right. In their own way," he couldn't help adding. Likewise, he couldn't help the sarcasm that punctuated the statement. "Our house looked like a spread out of *House & Garden,* if you must know. Twelve-foot Fraser fir in the ballroom, smaller trees in the foyer, living room and office. Presents wrapped in foil stacked up to the ceiling. Parties, visitors, carols on the stereo, wassail, eggnog, you name it. My family went the whole nine yards for Christmas."

"It sounds wonderful," she said with a warm smile. "I would have loved Christmas at your house."

He thought about the construction paper chains and the little plastic Christmas tree that Mindy had packed so carefully into one of the boxes. Even though she barely had two nickels to rub together, she'd done her best to make her ugly apartment look nice for the holiday. And for all the splash, splendor and sparkle of Christmas at the Atchisons, Mindy's decorations were so much more appealing. Because they were real. They were genuine. They had been inspired by love and a true affection for Christmas.

Not because she'd wanted to outdo her neighbors. Not because she'd wanted to impress her co-workers. Not because that was what everyone else in the neighborhood did, and by God the Atchisons weren't going to be left behind.

But Reed recalled his mother's incessant complaints about having too much to do at Christmas, especially for *other people,* and about all the leeching charities that kept demanding money, and how was she supposed to make time for a facial when she had to organize a Christmas Eve luncheon for God's sake, and oh, Reed, dear, this ornament you made in school simply does not go with the theme of the tree, so you won't mind if we hang it in back on the bottom where no one will see it, will you—there's a good boy.

He remembered his father's demands about how their Christmas party this year had better be a damned sight better than the Scofields' party had been, and just why the hell was he supposed to give gifts to everyone on his damned staff when everyone on his damned staff didn't work hard enough to deserve a lump of coal, and, Reed, just what the hell were you thinking to give me a bottle of Old Spice, even if you did pick it out and pay for it all by yourself?

"No you wouldn't," he told Mindy. "You wouldn't have liked Christmas at my house at all. There's a lot more to the holiday than big, beautiful trees with tinsel, mountains of presents, and buffet spreads."

He knew she couldn't possibly understand his objection, but there was no way he was going to dwell on his memories long enough to explain things to her. Simply put, he'd left all that behind him. And he wasn't interested in ever going back for a visit.

"You could still do a little tree," she said. "It wouldn't take up much room."

He studied her in silence for a moment, noting the hopeful, wistful little smile that curled her lips. "Don't bother, Mindy," he said softly. "It's nice of you to try but..." He gave a little shrug. "I'm a lost cause. Everybody will tell you the same."

Her lips parted almost imperceptibly, and her cheeks darkened with color. He thought she was going to say something to object, but she remained silent. Evidently, she finally believed him on that score, he thought, thinking he should feel happy that he'd gotten through to her. Instead, at realizing she now recognized him for exactly the kind of man he was, Reed only felt...empty. Bereft. As if, for a moment, he'd held something very wonderful and mystical in his hand only to have it brutally snatched away and smashed into a million pieces.

He took a few steps toward the front door, suddenly wanting

to be somewhere else. Someplace where there wasn't a woman gazing upon him as if she were a trusting little child, and he'd just laughingly told her there was no such thing as Santa Claus.

"There are plenty of groceries," he said as he made his escape. "I stocked the place this afternoon, with a little bit of everything. And you might want to get those leftovers out of the cooler and into the fridge before you go to bed. Still, you shouldn't go hungry." He grabbed the doorknob and turned it quickly to the right, jerking the door inward. Almost there, he thought. Almost…

"Reed…"

"There are extra blankets in the hall closet," he continued hastily, not wanting to hear that soft, unguarded note in her voice, "and toiletries in the bathroom cabinet. If there's anything I missed, write it down, and I'll pick it up for you tomorrow."

"Reed…"

"If it's okay, I'll come by on my lunch hour to check on you, unless you're going to be working."

She hesitated, then seemed to give up on whatever she'd wanted to tell him. "Evie has me down for the dinner shift tomorrow. I should be here until about three-thirty."

"Fine," he said in a voice that came out much rougher than he intended. "Fine," he reiterated, a bit more evenly this time. "I'll, uh…I'll call first."

"Fine," she echoed, her own voice sounding a bit hollow.

The hallway outside, the one that led to sweet escape, beckoned him, but for some reason, Reed lingered. She just looked so… And he just felt so… And there was just so much…

He squelched a thread of need that wound through him, tightening his fist on the doorknob. "Good night, Mindy," he said, still not moving.

"Good night, Reed. And thanks."

"No problem."

Go! a voice inside him shouted. And finally, finally, Reed listened. Stepping through the door, he tugged it closed behind him, the soft snick of the latch echoing loudly somewhere deep inside his soul. For a moment, he only stood there, still clinging to the doorknob, reluctant to leave, hesitant to stay. And he hated himself for feeling so ambivalent about…everything.

It was all this talk of Christmas, he thought. All this blithering and gushing about an overly romanticized holiday that could never possibly measure up to what all the troubadours, poets and television specials insisted it should be.

"Bah, humbug," he muttered to himself as he released the doorknob and forced himself to walk away.

Christmas. Who needed it anyway?

On the other side of the door, Mindy pressed her eye to the peephole and wondered why Reed was still hanging around. The fish eye distorted his image, so that she had no idea what he might be thinking or doing, but for some reason he lingered outside for several moments after he'd left.

Then, very quietly, she heard him say, "Bah, humbug." And she would have smiled, if he hadn't sounded so utterly desolate and so completely alone.

He did turn to leave then, and she watched him go until he rounded the corner at the end of the hall and was out of her line of vision. Ignoring the echo of melancholy inside her, she spun around and marveled once more at the place where she had landed—this vision from the magical land of interior decoration. She'd never in her life been around such sumptuous surroundings. The furnishings were elegant and masculine, reeking of money and sophistication. And even if they lacked a certain…humanity, a certain…soul, they were still rich, beautiful and indulgent.

She really shouldn't have come.

Even though she knew she hadn't had much choice, that she would, quite literally, have been on the streets had she not accepted Reed's offer, Mindy still couldn't quite quell the sensation that she'd made a terrible, terrible mistake. As had become her habit when she was doubting herself, she opened her hand over her belly, smoothing it over the life that grew within.

"I did this for you, kiddo," she said softly. "So you could be safe and healthy. I just hope it doesn't blow up in our faces."

Moving toward the first of the boxes holding all of her worldly possessions, Mindy decided not to think about that right now. Right now, she would take a bath and put on her pajamas, then check out the contents of the kitchen and maybe watch a movie on cable TV.

She smiled. It had been a long time since she'd watched television, period, let alone had the choices offered up by cable. She wondered if she'd missed "A Charlie Brown Christmas" or "Rudolph the Red-Nosed Reindeer" or *It's a Wonderful Life.* Then again, with cable, all the traditional Christmas shows would probably be repeated over and over and over again, ad nauseam, before the holiday finally arrived.

She just hoped she caught them every single time.

Pulling her flannel jammies out of the box, Mindy headed off to the bathroom, humming "Frosty the Snowman" under her breath as she went.

Once Reed had Mindy settled in her new place—or, rather, at his place—he figured he would stop worrying about her and that she would cease to be front and center in his brain. He assumed he would be able to go to work everyday and perform his job as well as always, and not have every other thought dwelling on what Mindy Harmon was doing. That he would exchange the usual pleasantries with the other doctors and nurses, and steal away for the occasional lunch or dinner with Seth—somewhere other than Evie's Diner, because the last thing he wanted was to give Mindy the impression he was worrying about her—just as he always did, and not worry about whether she was getting enough to eat.

He was wrong.

Because the realization that Mindy was living at his condo, amid his things, sleeping in his bed played havoc with Reed's

senses unlike anything ever had before. Instead of being com-
forted by the knowledge that she was safe and sound, eating
well and resting, taking better care of herself and her baby, he
felt agitated. Instead of feeling that he'd done enough for her,
he found that he only wanted to do more. Yes, by giving her
a place to stay rent-free, he'd enabled her to minimize her
hours at the diner, and by stocking food in the condo, he'd
made sure that she—and her baby—received the proper nutrition.

But those gestures just seemed so paltry. He should be doing
more.

Unfortunately, he wasn't sure what that *more* might be. He
only knew that something inside him told him that there was
still something Mindy needed, still something he could give
to her that he hadn't already, still something that would make
her life a little better, a little easier.

He just didn't know what that something was. And it was
driving him crazy, trying to figure it out.

So Reed did his best to forget about it, to put it from his
mind and focus instead on what was essential to life. His job.
His patients. His rounds at the hospital. Just because it was
Christmas outside didn't mean things slowed down any in the
medical field. On the contrary, for many departments, this time
of year brought on more work than ever.

But the Coronary Care Unit at Seton General didn't require
much overtime from him, thereby leaving him with his
thoughts more often than he cared to be left with them. Worse
than that, though, everywhere he turned, he saw evidence of
the holiday. The staff, making merry, had decorated the CCU
with tinsel and fake poinsettias, giving the unit a strangely
festive feel that it didn't normally have. The nurses and other
doctors seemed cheerier lately, and even the patients appeared
to be doing better than usual.

Only Reed remained unaffected by the seasonal changes.
Why should he feel cheery, after all? What was the point? He
still couldn't understand what the big deal was about Christmas. Really, when you got right down to it, December

shouldn't be any different from any other month of the year. The weather brought cold, dampness, and snow and slush that grew gray and dirty the longer it sat on the ground. The skies were thick and slate more often than not, preventing even the merest ray of sunlight to warm the earth.

Traffic compounded, thanks to an endless array of shoppers and people making the rounds of visiting, and the hustle and bustle was in no way conducive to a good humor. People spent more money than they could afford on gift giving, thereby multiplying a debt that in many cases was already crippling. And nothing seemed to get done, because few were in the mood to work. This time of year, drunk-driving fatalities were up, domestic violence was up, suicide rates were up, stress levels were up.

So really, all things considered, December and the holiday season were a nuisance, at best, a tragedy at worst. Why was Reed the only person who seemed to realize that? And why was everyone else so damned happy all the time?

And speaking of so damned happy, he thought as he glanced up from a patient's chart late one afternoon a week before Christmas, there went Seth. He sported a jaunty Santa Claus hat, had one arm around a patient, and the other around a nurse and was laughing his fool head off over something.

What did that guy find to be so happy about all the time? Reed wondered. It was as if the simple act of being alive just brought no end of fun for the man.

''Reed!'' he said when he glanced up and saw his friend. ''You're just the man I've been looking for. I'm having some people over to my place Friday night for a little preholiday gathering. You are, of course, invited.''

A few people to Seth generally meant anywhere from two dozen to two hundred, so Reed didn't immediately accept the offer. He wasn't comfortable in crowds, even among people he knew, and if the occasion was Christmas, well… He'd just as soon pass. Evidently, Seth realized that, because he bid a hasty farewell to the two women in his company and strode toward Reed with much purpose.

"You are *not* going to put me off on this," he vowed. "You don't get out enough and, as a result, you're turning into a real hermit crab these days."

Reed arched his eyebrows in silent affront.

"Uh...a crabby hermit?" Seth amended.

This time Reed arrowed his brows downward.

"Okay, look, you're just no fun anymore—not that you were such a barrel of monkeys to begin with, quite frankly—and I, for one, am growing tired of it."

"Then stop hanging around with me," Reed told him.

Seth gaped at him, aghast. "What and miss all your scintillating conversation? No way. Besides, the nurses like you better than me—go figure—and it's easier for me to meet women when I'm with you."

Now this was news to Reed. He rather thought he drove women away in, well, droves. "You're nuts," he told his friend.

"I'm afraid it's true," Seth insisted. "Women dig that dark, silent routine of yours."

"It's not a routine," Reed said.

"I *know,* that's what drives me crazy!" Seth exclaimed. "And women dig sincerity even more than they do that dark, silent routine."

Reed shook his head. "You are making absolutely no sense."

"Just come to my place on Friday, okay? Drinks at six, dinner at seven."

Reed couldn't quite mask his apprehension. "You're cooking?"

"Hell, no, I'm not cooking. What are you, nuts? I'm having the thing catered by a woman named Mitzi. Mitzi, Reed. Do you know how few women are named Mitzi these days?"

"Do I care?"

Seth's tongue fairly lolled out the side of his mouth as he replied, "You will when you meet...Mitzi. Wear a tie, okay?"

Reed made a face. "I'm liking this less and less with every new requirement."

Seth smiled, a very self-satisfied—and therefore very disturbing—smile. "Then you're going to love the final one," he said.

Reed narrowed his eyes. "What is it?"

Seth's smile turned downright smug as he began to walk away, and Reed soon found out why. Over his shoulder, he tossed out, "Bring a date. Everyone else is. And I don't want you to throw off the seating. It would put Mitzi in a very bad mood, and I don't want Mitzi in a bad mood."

Before Reed could fire off a retort, Seth was gone. And he thought to himself that Mitzi wasn't the only one who was going to be in a bad mood Friday night. Because there was no way Reed would be bringing a date. Not for Christmas. Not for anything.

Bah, humbug.

"You want me to go where?"

Mindy stood at the lunch counter in Evie's Diner and eyed Seth Mahoney, who sat on the stool directly opposite her, with much suspicion. She was certain she must have misheard. Because she could think of only one place on the planet where she would feel more uncomfortable than she did being alone in Reed Atchison's condo—and *uncomfortable* was exactly how she'd felt for the entire week that she'd been living there. But being at a party in Seth Mahoney's condo would be even worse.

Nevertheless, the blond M.D. was adamant. "Come on, Mindy. It'll be fun."

What was up with these doctors? she wondered. Why was she suddenly their best friend in the whole, wide world? Had somebody put something in the water at Seton General? Sheesh. "Thank you," she said as graciously as she could manage, "but I don't think I can make it. I have to work Friday night."

"Not to worry," he said. "I asked Donna if she'd cover for you, and she agreed. She felt it was the least she could do after revealing all your deep dark secrets to me and Reed that first night we came in.''

Mindy shook her head, but couldn't help smiling. ''That's very nice of Donna. But I can't afford to give up the money I'd make working a Friday night shift, so…'' She shrugged again. ''Thanks, but no thanks.''

She was surprised by how crestfallen he appeared to be over her decline of his offer.

''But it'll be fun,'' he told her, almost petulantly, she thought. ''You'll have a good time, I promise.''

''I wish I could, but I can't,'' she said. ''Besides, I don't have anything to wear.''

''Oh, now that's a really lame excuse,'' he told her.

''It's true,'' she insisted. ''I don't.''

He studied her for a long time in silence, then slowly shook his head, as if in disappointment. ''No money, no clothes… Mindy, you're positively pathetic.''

She gaped at him. ''I beg your pardon?''

''It's true,'' he said. ''A sorrier sight of self-pity I've never seen in my life.''

She gaped harder. ''I *beg* your pardon.''

''I mean, what kind of example will you be setting for your child if you make yourself out to be such a victim all the time? Have some pride, will ya?''

Had she been able to, Mindy would have gaped even *harder.* ''I *beg* your *pardon.*''

He sighed fitfully. ''Oh, well. I guess if the weak, pitiful act is the one you want your daughter or son to follow, it's none of *my* business. How's the chicken salad today?''

He had turned his attention to the menu without another thought, and Mindy found herself doing a slow burn at his easy dismissal of her. Which was strange, because she was the one who'd wanted to be dismissed, at least where a party invitation was concerned. When she withdrew her pencil from beneath her ponytail, she nearly snapped it in two, so rigidly, so angrily did she grip it in her fist. And her jaw ached with the tightness of clenching her teeth.

A victim? she repeated to herself as Seth perused the lunch choices. Pathetic? A sorry sight of self-pity? Weak? Pitiful? Her? Mindy Harmon?

I don't think so.

"What time do you want me to come over Friday?" she asked impulsively.

But Seth didn't even look up. "Oh, don't bother," he said. "Forget I asked. With your attitude, you'd probably just put a damper on the evening anyway. Nobody wants to be reminded of poor creatures like you at Christmas."

"Hey!"

Well, that, at least, got his attention. A little, at any rate. He did glance up from the menu. He looked totally bewildered when he did, but he did glance up. "What?" he asked innocently, seeming to be genuinely puzzled by her outburst.

"I am *not* a poor creature," she told him. "I'm *not* a victim. I'm *not* weak and pathetic. And I certainly wouldn't put a damper on your party."

"Mmm," Seth remarked before returning his attention to the menu.

When he said nothing more, she drummed her fingertips restlessly on the countertop and glared at the top of his head. "You know, I've been told that I'm actually a lot of fun at parties," she said.

He didn't look up. "Yeah, but you don't want to give up the money you'd make Friday. I understand."

"That's okay," she conceded grudgingly. "Donna could use the extra money, too. She's saving up to buy a Mustang."

Still reading the menu, he replied, "But, you don't have anything to wear. Don't worry about it. I don't know what I was thinking to ask in the first place."

She narrowed her eyes in menace, then realized the gesture would be lost on him, seeing as how he still wasn't looking at her. "Well, I do have this dress I wore when I was in Sam's cousin's wedding last Valentine's Day," she said. "It's really nice, and I've actually lost weight since then, and it has an

Empire waist, so my growing tummy wouldn't be a problem. It would probably fit."

He finally turned his head to the side enough to look at her out of the corner of his eye. "Well, I don't want you to do anything you don't want to do, Mindy. If you don't want to come to my party, just say so. It won't hurt my feelings. Much. I'll get over it. Someday."

Of course, she realized then that Seth was only stringing her along, and had been from the beginning with all that stuff about her being pathetic and a victim and all. She'd just risen to the bait, as he'd known she would. But dammit, Mindy wasn't a victim. She wasn't pathetic. And maybe—just maybe—she'd have fun at his party. It had been a long time since she'd had fun, she thought. And heaven knew she needed a break from the ordinary, everyday struggle of trying to survive.

When she didn't say anything more, Seth finally looked up from his menu to give her his full attention. And she saw that he really was a lot more hopeful and a lot less disinterested than he was letting on.

She folded her arms over her midsection and eyed him warily. "I know you've just been yanking my chain," she said quietly, "but a Christmas party sounds like fun. Thank you for inviting me. I'd love to come."

Eight

One thing about Seth, Reed noted the moment he stepped through his friend's front door, he knew how to throw a party, particularly one for the holiday. A six-foot Christmas tree spattered with white lights, silver tinsel and seemingly hundreds of color-coordinated ornaments sparkled in the corner of the living room, near French doors that led to a light-bedecked balcony beyond. A jazzy saxophone rendition of "Have Yourself a Merry Little Christmas" wafted from the stereo, not quite drowning out the dozen or so guests who mingled throughout the place amid a continuous murmur. The aroma of red wine and roast beef tinted the air, completing the environment of holiday cheer.

For some reason, Reed was nearly overcome by a poignant feeling of emptiness that he couldn't quite understand. A feeling that somehow, somewhere, he was missing out on something very important, something that other people enjoyed, but that he couldn't understand. So, as he generally did when such puzzling emotions ran through him, he opted to ignore it.

It looked to be a nice party, and he was genuinely happy that he had come. Seth's talent for entertaining no doubt stemmed from the fact that he was so damned genial and outgoing, and so well-liked by everyone in the western—and hell, probably the eastern, too—hemisphere. Okay, so maybe there was something to be said for warm qualities, Reed thought grudgingly. On the right person.

"Glad you could make it," Seth said, straightening a necktie that was decorated with little images of holly, a design that matched the festive boutonniere in his dark lapel. "Though I notice you didn't bring a date. Imagine my shock and surprise."

"I never said I'd bring a date," Reed reminded him, handing his host his overcoat, tugging at his own dark suit and berry-colored tie, the one concession he'd been willing to make for the holiday party theme. Actually, he had thought about inviting a guest—oh, say…Mindy, for example—but something had stopped him every time he'd picked up the phone to call her.

Except for that day after he'd helped her get settled in at his condo, when he'd checked to make sure everything was okay, he hadn't seen or spoken to her. He'd *wanted* to see and speak to her, but he hadn't thought it would be a good idea, what with all those bewitching, bothering and bewildering—in fact, all the downright *bizarre*—thoughts and feelings he'd had muddling his brain and guts lately.

So he'd avoided both his condo and the diner where she worked. The memory of that kiss they'd shared the first night in her apartment was still much too fresh—and much too confusing—in his memory, and he didn't think it would be prudent to repeat it. Mindy was in a vulnerable, precarious situation right now, and he didn't see any reason to contribute to it by exploring whatever strange…stuff…might—or might not—be going on between them.

Whatever had caused them to turn to each other that night, whether it was a shared feeling of loneliness or wistfulness or something else entirely, he was sure it had been inspired by some kind of holiday weirdness and nothing more. People's emotions always ran amok this time of year, only to settle down once the holidays drew to a close. Reed was no exception. And he was confident that whatever was simmering between the two of them wouldn't last much beyond Christmas. Mindy had enough to worry about right now without a doomed and pretty much phony holiday romance adding to the mix.

"Yeah, I know you didn't promise," his friend replied with one of those knowing—and very annoying—smiles, bringing Reed's thoughts back to the fore. "And I knew you wouldn't bring a date. So I took the liberty of inviting one for you."

Reed emitted a defeated sound and closed his eyes in disbelief. Why had he not seen that coming from a mile away? he asked himself. How could he possibly have thought that Seth would let him come to this party stag? God only knew who the poor unsuspecting woman was that his host had invited to be Reed's companion for the evening. He just hoped she had a good sense of humor. She was going to need it.

Unless maybe Seth invited… Uh-oh.

As if conjured by the very thought, the doorbell rang, and Seth's bright smile went supernova. "Why, I'll bet that's her now."

Uh-oh, uh-oh, uh-oh…

They had taken a few steps into the richly appointed condo—Seth had hired the same decorator Reed had—but hesitated at the soft chime of the bell. Reed took another step backward as Seth reached for the doorknob, moving himself out of the way of the entry…and curbing the instinct that commanded him to hurtle himself through the French doors that led to the patio and scale down the side of the building like Spiderman.

The door opened toward him, so he couldn't see who was standing on the other side—not that he needed to see, because he was already absolutely certain that Seth had blindsided him by inviting Mindy to be his date. Then Reed noticed the look on Seth's face as he greeted his guest and decided that he was wrong. Because judging by the way Seth's jaw dropped to the ground at the sight of the newcomer, whoever it was had commanded the other man's attention in a big way.

Which was saying something, because Seth Mahoney took the label of ladies' man to new heights. There wasn't a woman alive he hadn't wanted—or tried—to seduce, usually with better than average results. He found beauty and grace in all things female—regardless of race, color, creed, species or planetary origin—and appreciated more than most men did all those puzzling qualities that made the fairer sex so alien to any normal-thinking male.

So for Seth to react like this meant that the woman who had just arrived must be some piece of goddesslike work indeed, a supreme specimen of womanhood. She must be, as Seth was wont to say, extremely elegant, sumptuously sophisticated, bountifully built and ferociously fair. She must be of sound—very sound—body, if not mind. She must be—

"Mindy?"

Mindy? Yes, that was indeed, quite definitely, Mindy Harmon who strode through the door, glancing about nervously, as if she expected someone to jump out and yell, "Boo!" Reed didn't realize he'd spoken her name out loud, however, until she glanced over at him and blushed.

The color tinting her cheeks was just a shade lighter than the dress she wore, which was a deep, red-as-a-rose-petal velvet, revealed in increments as Seth helped her out of her coat. Reed decided it might be best if he just ignored the stab of jealousy that pierced him at the sight of his best friend performing that very gesture. Especially since the appearance of Mindy provided him with an infinitely more alluring, if not exactly calming, sight to behold.

The neckline of her dress scooped low above—and lovingly hugged—her breasts, revealing their dusky, and surprisingly ample, swells, before cascading down to just above her knees in a sweep of loose-fitting fabric. Sheer black stockings covered her legs, ending in black ballet flats decorated with silky red roses. Around her neck, she had tied a black satin ribbon, and in the sweep of loose curls atop her head she had tucked a spray of tiny satin roses, the same red color as her dress. The same red color as—

—her mouth.

Oh, her mouth, he thought, his gaze riveting there of its own free will. Reed hadn't realized how full her lips were, how lush and generous was the swell of the lower one, how perfectly, exquisitely bowed was the curve of the upper one. And when those lips parted fractionally, as if she needed to catch her breath, his heart began to hammer hard in his chest, his own breath halting somewhere deep within him.

"Hi," she said quietly, the word coming out as scarcely more than a sigh.

She smiled a little shyly, and the breath that had hesitated inside Reed suddenly squeezed from his lungs in a long, lusty whoosh.

"Fancy meeting you here," she added, an almost imperceptible tremble shaking her voice.

"Uh…" he began eloquently. But no more words—or even sounds—were forthcoming, because, to be perfectly honest, his brain had turned into pudding.

Beside him, Seth laughed. "Mindy, I think you've rendered the old man speechless. Congratulations. I knew it was a good idea to invite you." Without warning, he pulled a sprig of mistletoe from nowhere and held it over her head, then leaned forward and kissed her chastely on the cheek. "Merry Christmas, sweetheart. I'm glad you could come."

Reed watched his friend's playful actions and wanted, quite frankly, to kill him. Slowly and with great deliberation. With his bare hands. Twice. Somehow, though, he refrained. Such an act would, no doubt, ruin Christmas. At least, for Seth's parents.

"Gimme that," Reed said instead. He snatched the mistletoe out of Seth's fingers, then tucked it into the breast pocket of his jacket for safekeeping. "This could be a lethal weapon in your hands. No doubt the authorities have outlawed it in New Jersey, Pennsylvania *and* Delaware, where you're concerned. Probably the whole eastern seaboard, to boot. *And* the mid-Atlantic states," he added, not quite as an afterthought.

Seth's smile told Reed he knew exactly what had generated his reaction, and it *wasn't* any concern for the safety of American women east of the Mississippi. But, thankfully, his friend said nothing to expose him. "Come on in, Mindy," he said instead. "We've been waiting for you. It ought to be an interesting night."

That was an understatement, Reed thought as he watched Seth close the door and move toward the crowd of guests on the other side of the living room. A few people spilled over into the dining area and kitchen, leaving Reed and Mindy alone near the front door.

"You look..." He couldn't think of a single word that would do her justice, except maybe, "Wow."

She chuckled a little self-consciously at the sentiment, blushing again, her gaze darting away for a moment, then back to his face. And then, after a moment, she said, "You look pretty wow yourself."

Once again, his brain failed him, because he could think of absolutely nothing to say in response. Man, all those years of school—private school, prep school, college, med school, you name it—yet as he stood there staring at Mindy, the only thing running through his mind was...*woof.* It was just that as he stood there staring at Mindy, something as mundane as talking—or thinking—began to seem like such a waste of time.

"It, um, it was nice of Seth to invite me," she continued, stirring Reed some from his reverie. "I mean, he didn't have to. I certainly wasn't expecting anything like this."

Although somewhere deep within Reed's system, he did, in fact, grasp the concept of conversation, recalled that there was a give-and-take to it, remembered that it involved more than one person, he couldn't quite come up with what his part of the task should be. So, again, he only stood silent gazing at Mindy, marveling at the way her face seemed softer and rounder than it had the last time he'd seen her. And at how the pale blond curls dancing about her face looked like silk. And at how her eyes fairly sparkled with laughter and light.

And at how he wanted so very badly to kiss her again.

"After all, *you're* the one who's supposed to be doing a good deed for me," she finally concluded, carrying her side, at least, of the conversation quite nicely.

When he understood the remark, Reed finally, finally snapped out of the deep, druglike trance into which he'd tumbled while gazing at Mindy. Good deed, he prompted himself. Right. Now he remembered. He was supposed to be doing a good deed for Mindy Harmon. Not mooning and drooling all over her.

"Yes, well," he began, injecting a lightness into his voice he was nowhere close to feeling, "Seth is a regular party animal. Any excuse to have people over, he'll take it. Especially if those people happen to be female."

Mindy smiled, looking relieved that Reed was, in fact, an articulate human being, after all. "He is rather charming, isn't he?"

That, Reed thought, was open to debate. However, the whys and wherefores of Seth Mahoney's dubious charm were the last things he wanted to be discussing this evening with Mindy. So in response to her question—which really hadn't called for an answer anyway, had it?—Reed crooked his elbow and held it out to her. "Shall we mingle?" he asked.

She chuckled. "That sounds like a very good idea. Lead on."

Mindy had always been of the opinion that the word *mingle* sort of indicated an action of moving from one person to another during the course of the evening. But she seemed to keep gravitating toward Reed throughout the entirety of Seth's party. Or maybe, she thought with an odd, wistful hopefulness, Reed kept gravitating toward her. In either case, they seemed to be pretty much joined at the elbow until dinner—and then even during the meal, because Seth had assigned them places next to each other.

At first, Mindy hadn't been sure she'd be comfortable sitting so close to Reed, but she quickly decided it was for the best. Had she not been seated beside him, she would have been constantly looking for—and at—him. And looking at Reed, dressed in his extremely sexy dark suit and tie, his brown eyes warmed by some soft emotion that she was absolutely sure she was imagining, was just too dangerous for her to manage for any length of time.

Surely her fascination with him tonight resulted only from the fact that she had never dated a suit-wearing man, she mused. Sam had been a laborer, as had been most of her boyfriends before Sam entered her life. One or two had held jobs that required uniforms, but none had ever been required to dress up. Now she decided there was something infinitely appealing about a man in a suit. Especially a man like Reed.

Especially Reed.

The dark wool jacket stretched taut over his broad shoulders, and even the baggy trousers couldn't mask the well-built legs beneath. His shirt was pristine white beneath a necktie that was the color of a ripe winter apple, both hues offsetting his dark good looks quite nicely.

But what was most alluring was how comfortably he wore the garments. And maybe, really, that was the secret to his magnetism—he was supremely confident in himself and his place in the world. For someone like Mindy, who had never quite been sure where, exactly, her place in the scheme of things lay, his utter certainty of himself was very attractive.

And his tushie wasn't bad, either.

She had missed him—and, okay, his tushie, too—during the week that had just passed. His condo was comfortable enough but it felt empty somehow without him there. Everywhere she looked, she was confronted by his things, his possessions, his stuff. But Reed was nowhere among them.

In more ways than one, really. For a man who professed not to "do" cooking, he owned a lot of gourmet cookware. And in spite of his ability to wear suits well, like the two hanging in his closet, he seemed to be much more at ease in the jeans and sweaters she'd seen him wear more frequently. The handful of CDs in his collection were fairly bland background music, and the books lining a few shelves were all medical texts and copies of best-selling nonfiction.

Of course, his condo was only a temporary residence, she reminded herself. The majority of his things would be in his home on the Main Line. She knew she shouldn't expect the condo to offer her many snippets of insight into the man himself. But even at that, somehow, she knew none of it was in the least indicative of the man he really was beneath.

And Mindy missed that man. She missed him a lot. Those five nights in a row they'd spent sharing dinner at her apartment seemed almost like a dream now. She hadn't understood at the time how important those occasions had been to her. She hadn't realized how lonely her life had become until Reed had stepped in to bring companionship. But that companionship had been far too brief. And she wished she knew what to do to bring him back again. Not to stay, necessarily. Just…to visit. For a while. Was that so much to ask?

She bumped his elbow with hers as she reached for her water glass, and he glanced up to mumble an apology. And when he did, in that stark, crystalline moment, something occurred to Mindy that was both very wonderful and very troubling. If she wasn't careful, she realized, she could quite easily fall in love with Reed Atchison. In some ways, she was already more than halfway there. Even though she'd known him only a matter of weeks—days, really—she sensed in him a kinship of sorts, something the two of them shared that went beyond simple camaraderie.

She had no idea what that might be, but there it was all the same. Something in Reed spoke to something in her, and the recognition of that soothed a turbulence inside her she hadn't until this moment realized was there. He made her feel good. He made her feel safe. He made the world feel right. Being with him, she experienced a sense of peace and well-being unlike anything she had ever known before. He was a nice man with a good heart, and she'd met so very few of those in her life.

Even though Mindy always looked for the best in others, she wasn't so naive that she always found it. There were some people, she knew, who didn't give a fig for anyone other than themselves, some people who were just downright mean. There were those who were disinterested, those who were indifferent, those who were utterly malcontent. It did, after all, take all kinds to make a world.

But there were good people out there, too, and those were the ones she clung to as the norm. Unfortunately, the norm seemed to be coming fewer and farther between these days. Reed, she had detected from the start, was a very good example of a decent human being. Yet he continuously insisted that he was unmoved by the plight of others, that he was convinced people were no good at heart, that a season like Christmas only brought out the worst in everyone.

Why?

She couldn't begin to imagine. But if he were genuinely uncaring, genuinely cold, genuinely unmoved by the plight of others, then he would have taken her at her word and left her alone. He would have found some other way—some far less personal way—to pay off his bet with Seth. He wouldn't have brought her dinner all those nights. He wouldn't have kept insisting she use his place for as long as she needed it. He wouldn't have kissed her so tenderly and with such need.

He wouldn't keep smiling at her, and gazing at her, as if she were his last chance in a world gone sour.

The more Mindy thought about him—and heaven knew she'd spent *a lot* of time thinking about Reed this week—the more intrigued by him she became. And the more intrigued by him she became, the more she wanted to figure him out. What lay beneath his gruff exterior? she wondered. Besides that heart of gold?

Okay, so maybe his heart was a bit tarnished, she conceded as she watched him now. There was no reason it couldn't be polished up a bit. Why, it probably wouldn't take much effort at all to have it shining like the brightest beacon in the sky. And after all, it *was* Christmas. Bright beacons in the sky were by no means unheard-of. Stars were all the rage this time of year.

"I, uh…I noticed you cleaned up your plate," he said, dipping his head in that direction.

She followed his gaze and smiled. "It was very, very good."

"And you, evidently, were very, very hungry."

She leaned back in her chair, inhaled a deep, satisfied breath, and spread both hands open over her expanding tummy. "We both were," she told him.

Reed watched her action, and a look came over his face that was…very strange, she decided. There was wistfulness there, almost longing. And a warm, wonderful sense of peace, too, she noted. She could feel it emanating from him as clearly as she would feel his hand, if he reached out to touch her.

"Do you ever feel the baby move?" he asked, his gaze still settled on her midsection.

The question surprised her, but she told herself it shouldn't. "A few times," she said. "It happened more than once before I figured out what it was. It feels…"

"Like what?" he asked, glancing up at her face, his lips curled into a smile that was…very sweet.

"Interesting," she told him. "It feels interesting. A soft little flutter, like butterfly wings inside, or little fingers. It almost tickles."

He shook his head slowly, dropping his gaze back to the hands she had splayed over her belly. "I can't imagine. Even as a physician, I'm pretty much awed and overwhelmed by the whole reproductive process. It really is a miracle."

She chuckled. "That's your medical opinion?"

He thought about it for a moment, then nodded. "Yup. It is."

When his gaze met hers again, however, his amusement faded, to be replaced by something Mindy could only liken to the awe he had described. Unexpectedly, he lifted his hand toward her face, then hesitated for a moment before twining a single strand of hair around his forefinger. And all the while, his dark eyes were fixed on hers, as if he couldn't quite believe she was real.

"You're going to have a baby, Mindy," he said softly.

She smiled. "Yeah, I kinda already knew that."

He smiled, too, a bit less certainly. "No, I mean, it's just so incredible that you are. That there's a life in there, growing, and in a few months it will be a person. A tiny little human being that *you* are responsible for creating."

She swallowed hard, unable to look away from his face, even though she knew to continue gazing at him was probably *not* a very good idea. "Well, I did have a little help in that department," she said softly. "I didn't do it *all* by myself."

"But you're the one who's nurturing that tiny form," he said. "You're the one who's growing it. That baby is relying on *you* to give it life. When you think about that, it's pretty humbling. For a man, I mean. We can't do that. We can only sit back and watch it happen."

"Maybe you can't grow a child in the early stages," she said. "But once the baby is born, men can be just as nurturing as women. They can grow a child just as well as a woman could."

He shook his head. "No, that isn't true at all," he stated, quite adamantly.

His utter certainty surprised her. "Why do you say that?" she asked.

"Men just don't operate that way," he said.

"Some men don't," she agreed. "But some women don't, either. Being a good parent isn't a gender issue, Reed. It's an issue over whether one human being can love and care for another human being, that's all."

"You make it sound so simple."

She shrugged. "It is simple."

"You say that because you aren't afraid."

She couldn't help her laughter. "Oh, please. You can't imagine how scared I get sometimes. Ever since finding out about being pregnant, I've been terrified that something will go wrong, that the baby won't be healthy, that I'll do something to hurt it, that I'll be a terrible mother, that I won't be able to—''

"No," he interrupted her gently, "I meant you aren't afraid to love someone."

Mindy had no idea what to say in response, so she said nothing. She only gazed at Reed in wonder, wishing she knew what had happened to him to make him say and feel the things he did.

"You'll be a good mother, Mindy," he told her, oblivious to her thoughts.

She paused before saying what she wanted to say to that, worried that he might misconstrue her meaning. Then she thought, *What the heck.* There was no reason to hide her feelings from him.

She lifted one hand from her belly and moved it toward the table, covering his hand with sure fingers. "And you'd be a wonderful father," she told him, smiling what she hoped was an encouraging smile. "Any child would be lucky to call you Daddy."

His entire face went slack at her admission, as if he simply could not believe she had said what she had. At first, Mindy worried that he had indeed misunderstood, that he thought she was offering him the position of father to her child, when nothing could be further from the truth. Yes, she hoped to find a man someday who would claim both her and her child as his own. But she was fairly certain that man wouldn't be Reed Atchison.

As much as she might wish it could be.

But she realized he hadn't misconstrued her meaning at all when he told her, "You say that because you don't know me very well. I'd be a lousy father."

She shook her head. "I say that because I probably know you better than you know yourself."

He swallowed hard, and she watched as his throat worked

over the gesture. He was obviously unnerved by what she'd said. "You barely know me at all," he replied roughly.

Her fingers tightened on his. "We may have only made each other's acquaintance a couple of weeks ago, but it's been long enough for me to know."

He narrowed his eyes at her in clear confusion. "To know what?"

But Mindy only softened her smile, tucking her fingers more closely under his. Then she turned to her host, whom she found studying her and Reed with *much* interest from the other end of the table, a *huge* smile splitting his handsome features.

"I cleaned my plate," she told him. "Does that mean I get to have dessert?"

Seth laughed. "Can you handle a chocolate cheesecake?"

She nodded enthusiastically. "Oh, yes. But what's everyone else going to have?"

A wave of warm laughter ran up the entire table, even though Mindy had only been half joking. She was ravenous tonight. Even having consumed more than her fair share of dinner, she still had room for more than her fair share of dessert. Funny, how her appetite had been nearly unquenchable since Reed had started coming around. She'd gained seven very welcome pounds in the last two weeks. Much of it was thanks to being able to stuff herself silly on all the leftovers and groceries lying around. But much of it was also because she wasn't as worried about the future as she used to be.

She knew it probably wasn't a good idea to fall into a habit of complacency. She didn't want to rely on Reed any longer than she had to. And she certainly didn't want to take him for granted. Even though she couldn't mistake the odd ripples of attraction running between them, she wasn't so foolish as to think they were the result of anything other than some strange need Reed had to take care of her for now.

She didn't question why he had that need. Maybe it was because he was lonely. Maybe it was because he hadn't had anyone to care for in his past. Maybe it was because it was

Christmas. Whatever the reason for it, they were both bene-fiting from it.

For now.

But she knew better than to think it would continue forever. Still, that didn't mean she couldn't enjoy it while it lasted, did it? As long as she didn't let herself get in too deep. As long as she didn't let things go too far.

And naturally, Mindy thought, she would never let that hap-pen. She could keep her distance from Reed Atchison until after Christmas, until she found a place of her own. She could.

She would just make it a rule.

Nine

Rules were made to be broken, Reed thought as he walked Mindy to the door of her—his—condo later that evening. Or rather, later that *night,* he immediately corrected himself. Evening had passed into night some time ago—it was well past midnight now. But getting back to the rule thing—as reluctant as he was to do so—he tried to reassure himself that he hadn't done anything wrong this evening in breaking so many of his own rules, because…well…rules were made to be broken. Right?

Right.

So it was no big deal that Reed had broken a few. Or even several. Or more.

First, he'd broken his rule about not having more than one glass of wine with dinner. But having to gaze into Mindy's limitless green eyes all evening and having to hear her say some of the things she'd said, well… A second glass of wine hadn't seemed like such a big deal, especially since he'd consumed so much food with and after it. And especially since his adrenal gland, among others, had been working overtime from the moment he'd laid eyes on Mindy in that dress. He'd stopped at two glasses, he reminded himself. As much as he'd wanted to down a few—dozen—more.

But he'd also broken that rule he'd made about not engaging in anything other than idle chitchat with Mindy. Chitchat, hell, he thought morosely. They'd talked about their *feelings,* for God's sake. Their *emotions.* She'd even gone so far at one point after dinner as to tell him he'd be a good father. A good father. Him. Reed Atchison.

Right.

Not that he'd ever believe something like that, but it had been subject matter he really, really, *really* didn't want to broach. Not with anyone. And certainly not with a pregnant woman.

Which brought up another rule he'd broken tonight, the one about never, ever, under any circumstances, discussing parenting stuff with *anyone.* Even though he and Mindy had only briefly skirted that topic, they'd come too close for comfort. Reed didn't like to talk about parenting. Not any potential parenting he might give in the future—which was pretty much unlikely—and certainly not about any parenting he had received himself in the past—which was pretty much nonexistent. His folks had been cool toward everyone, their emotional responses to others tepid at best. And their own son had been included in that. But Reed wasn't the kind of man who would discuss such a thing with someone else. Especially someone like Mindy.

And then there was the biggie. Rule *numero uno.* He'd broken that sucker into about a million billion pieces this evening. That was the one where he'd promised himself he wouldn't look at Mindy as anything other than a nice young woman— a nice young *pregnant* woman—who needed a helping hand. He'd told himself he would only act as her patron, her sponsor, her knight in shining armor, a hero of sorts who was there to pull her out of trouble when she needed him. But nothing more than that. Nevertheless, that rule had gone zinging out the window the moment he'd laid eyes on her in that dress.

That dress. He still couldn't take his eyes off of that dress, as evidenced by the fact that he was staring at it right now. It obviously wasn't meant for maternity wear, in spite of its loose-fitting body, because the designer hadn't provided for a woman's more generous proportions in the uh, upper torso, that came with pregnancy. As Mindy shrugged off her coat, her breasts fairly spilled from the scooped neckline, and Reed squeezed his eyes shut tight against the image.

Too late. Because that image was indelibly printed at the forefront of his brain, and he figured it was going to be some time before he could erase it completely. Slowly, experimentally, he opened one eye, and was thankful to see Mindy's back turned to him as she hung her coat in the closet. He told himself this would be a good time to say good-night and get the hell outta Dodge, but instead of taking a step backward, out into the hallway, he strode forward instead, closing the door behind him.

Mindy spun around when he did, surprise etched on her features for a moment, before being replaced with a look of unmistakable pleasure.

"I could fix us some coffee," she said. "Decaf, if you don't mind."

"Sounds great," he told her, cursing himself for being too weak to beat a hasty retreat. Some heroic knight in shining armor he was turning out to be. Couldn't even run blindly away at the first sign of trouble. Sheesh.

"There are some Christmas cookies that I made, too," she said.

He smiled, thinking it was nice that she'd baked a batch of cookies. That just seemed like such a perfect little mother-to-be activity. But his smile fell some when she opened a cabinet and pulled down, not one, not two, not three, but *six* plastic containers. *Big* plastic containers. He hadn't even realized he *had* six plastic containers, big or otherwise. There must have been twelve dozen cookies in there, at least.

"Well, my, my, my," he said as she wrestled the top off of the first container. "Haven't we been a busy little bee this week?"

When she glanced up, he could see that she didn't understand what he was talking about.

So he added, "You weren't kidding when you said you were very, very hungry tonight."

Only then did she realize what he was getting at. She took in the six big containers and smiled back at him, a shy, self-conscious little smile that tied his heart in knots. "I've had a lot of time on my hands this week," she said softly. "Thanks to your generosity, I don't have rent to pay this month. And with the return of my damage deposit, I have enough money so that I don't feel compelled to work so many hours right now. Not that I could anyway," she added meaningfully, "seeing as how, even though Christmas is only a week away, Evie has insisted she just doesn't need me to work so many shifts, something I have a strange feeling is all your doing…"

"Who me? I have no idea what you're talking about," he lied smoothly.

He had, in fact, asked Evie if she could cut Mindy some slack where her shifts were concerned, considering her condition, and Evie had happily complied. She was of the opinion herself that Mindy worked too much but she hadn't had the heart to shorten or lessen her shifts, because she'd known her employee needed the money, and Mindy had pretty much insisted on the extra hours. Now that she'd received a reprieve in the form of Reed's patronage—or whatever the hell it was—Evie had been all too eager to go along with his request.

Mindy, however, threw him a look that told him she didn't buy his innocent act for a minute. But she didn't exactly seem upset that he would go behind her back that way. She only shrugged a bit negligently. "And it's Christmas," she added. "I wanted to enjoy at least some of the holiday. And I really do like to bake. I just haven't had the opportunity lately."

Meaning she hadn't been able to afford all the ingredients, Reed thought. But he didn't voice his assumption out loud.

Nevertheless, she seemed to know exactly what he was thinking. With another small shrug, she said, "Since you're saving me a month's rent—maybe more—I didn't see any reason why I couldn't splurge a little."

Splurge, he thought. To some of his friends, splurging would be going for the Range Rover instead of the Jeep Grand Cherokee. For Mindy, splurging was buying flour, sugar and butter.

"I'm going to take some of them to work," she added in her defense, "and I thought, if you wanted to, you could take some to the hospital for your friends."

That was a pretty nice thing for her to do, Reed thought, and he would have taken her up on her offer in a heartbeat. Except that he didn't have enough "friends" at the hospital to even warrant one dozen cookies, let alone the number she'd provided for him.

"Thanks," he said in spite of that. "I'll put some in the nurses' break room."

He was about to say something else, but she lifted the lid from the largest of the containers and his mouth began to water at the site he beheld inside. "Oooh, I *love* those," he said of the chocolate-oatmeal-peanut butter no-bake cookies. "Our housekeeper, Mrs. Cartwright, used to make them at Christmas time. I haven't had one for years."

Mindy chuckled as she scooped three good-sized cookies out of the container and placed them on a paper towel on the counter in front of Reed. He ate the first one in two bites but decided to slow down and enjoy the second, taking three out of that one. The sweet cookies melted in his mouth, tasting as magical as only chocolate and peanut butter mixed together could, and he didn't think he'd ever have a more transcendental experience in his life, even if he climbed to the very highest mountaintop in Tibet to consort with the Dalai Lama. Not unless the Dalai Lama had a big plastic container full of chocolate-oatmeal-peanut butter cookies, at any rate.

"Hey, save room for some nut nibbles," Mindy said, laughing. "And stained glass cookies and shortbread and icing cookies and—"

"Mindy," Reed interrupted her after he'd polished off the third cookie and swooped in for a fourth, "you really should be taking it easier than you are. Not that I object to cookies, mind you," he added, lifting the fourth in salute. "But I was hoping you'd get some rest this week. That was kind of the point to having Evie cut back on your shifts."

"So you *were* responsible for that," she charged. Somehow, though, there was no menace in her voice when she said it.

"Guilty," he confessed. "But in my medical opinion, you need to slow down. Otherwise, you're risking your health *and* the baby's."

She eyed him curiously. "Are you forming a medical opinion about that?" she asked.

He shook his head. "No. I'm speaking as your friend. As someone who cares about what happens to you."

She nodded slowly in understanding, but there was something sad and lonely in the gesture, something that didn't sit well with Reed. Before he could figure out what it was, though, she sighed heavily, scrunched up her shoulders again, then let them drop.

"I've been resting," she told him. "I just feel restless sometimes, too. It's strange being here all by myself, with Christmas just around the corner. I feel as if there's so much I should be doing, so many things that I used to do for the holiday that don't need doing this year, because I'm alone. I mean, I see everyone at work everyday and everything, but it's not like…"

When her voice trailed off before she completed the statement, Reed asked, "It's not like what?"

She sighed heavily. "It's not like being with loved ones. With family. Christmas is a time for family and friends—or at least it should be—and this is my first Christmas alone. Not that my family was ever anything out of *It's a Wonderful Life* or anything, but still. It just feels weird this year, that's all."

He studied her in thoughtful silence for a moment. Of

course, he'd known that about her already, the fact that she had no one in her life. Not only had she already told him that, but he'd witnessed for himself her solitary status. Still, it only now occurred to him what that would mean to someone like her, who was naturally outgoing and gregarious. "There really is no one?" he asked.

She shook her head. "I never knew my father. And my mother's been gone for a long time now. She had a sister, but my Aunt Margaret has lived on the West Coast since before I was born, and I don't really know her at all. My in-laws and I never got along very well, and after Sam…" She hesitated, dropping her gaze to the cookie in her hand, the one she'd been slowly and methodically breaking into itty-bitty pieces. "Well," she finally started up again, "they became downright hostile toward me after he died. They blame me for his death. Anyway—"

"They blame you for their son's death?" Reed asked, incredulous. "You told me he was a drunk-driving fatality. How could they possibly blame you for that?"

She expelled a single small, sad sound, broke off a few more crumbs of cookie and avoided his gaze. "They think if I hadn't gotten myself pregnant, then Sam wouldn't have started drinking again. They've even speculated that the baby I'm carrying isn't Sam's. They've pretty much made it clear that they don't want to be a part of our lives, and that I shouldn't look to them for support."

"That's crazy," Reed said angrily, a red haze of outrage and retribution swelling up inside him. "How dare they even suggest that you—"

"Look, can we talk about something else?" she interrupted him, dropping what was left of the cookie onto a napkin with its remnants. "I've put all that behind me. Truly, I have. I need to look to the future now. The baby and I will make it fine on our own. I do wish he—or she—would have a little bit bigger family, though. I think it's important for a child to have a strong support system."

Because she hadn't had one of her own, Reed thought. He

should have realized she'd feel that way. And he should have anticipated her feelings of loneliness, too. It hadn't occurred to him that solitude at Christmas would hit her so hard, because he was so used to it himself. He'd been a late-life surprise for his parents, and both had passed away within months of each other when Reed was in his twenties. He'd pretty much spent the last decade's worth of Christmases alone, so he was more or less used to it.

Used to it, he echoed coolly to himself. Right. As if anyone ever got *used to* being alone. Ah, well. Life was what it was, and no amount of regretting it was going to change things. 'Tis the season to be solitary, he thought. Always had been, always would be. Just because his parents weren't around anymore didn't make the holiday any less lonely than it had been when they were alive.

Of course, he didn't have to be alone this Christmas, he thought. There was Mindy. Maybe the two of them could—

No, they couldn't, he immediately corrected himself. No way. He would not use her as a buffer against the isolation. She deserved better than that.

"For what it's worth, it gets easier," he told her. "Being alone at Christmas, I mean. The first few years, the house feels empty, and you do sort of feel at loose ends. But ultimately, you find ways to fill the silence, ways to fill the time." But not the emptiness, he thought. That pretty much hangs around forever. Still, it wasn't like having family around had made a difference there.

"You sound like you're speaking from experience," she said.

He shrugged philosophically. "Maybe I am."

"You don't spend the holidays with your family? I mean, I know you said you're an only child and that your folks are gone," she added, "but surely there are other people who'd love to have you for the holidays. Aunts? Uncles? Cousins?"

He shook his head. "I don't really have much family left, per se. My folks have been gone for more than ten years now, so I've lost touch with the handful of aunts, uncles and cousins who are nearby. The rest are pretty scattered." And those who weren't scattered were pretty obnoxious, he added to himself.

She leaned forward, bracing her forearms on the countertop, lacing her fingers loosely together. Although she had no way of realizing it, the action brought into stark focus the lush swells of her breasts, the dusky valley between, the creamy skin that just beckoned for a man's touch. Reed forced himself to look away, toward the French doors leading to the dark balcony beyond, doors that were limned around the edges with fog from the warmth of the room. But the action hadn't come quickly enough to prevent his pulse from tripling, nor to halt the jarring heat of desire that rocked him.

"I'm sorry about your family," she said softly.

Me, too, he thought. But his regret was for something completely different from what she was voicing. Mindy was sorry his family was gone. Reed was sorry that they'd never really been there to begin with. Not in the way that he'd wanted them to be. Not in the way he'd needed them.

"You know," she said, her voice soft, tentative, "if you're not doing anything Christmas Eve, you're more than welcome to spend it here. It's your place after all. And I certainly wouldn't mind the company."

Her invitation was offered carelessly, as if she were simply throwing it out there for the most casual of reasons, but somehow Reed detected an underlying importance to it that she didn't want him to see. Her voice was edged with a tremble of uncertainty, as if she were afraid of hearing his answer, no matter what it turned out to be.

Still gazing at the French doors, noting the way he and Mindy were reflected in the dark glass—and the fact that they looked quite nice together, really—Reed bit back the ready agreement that swelled up inside him. *Yes!* he wanted to shout. *I'll be here! You can count on me!* But he knew it would be foolish to say something like that. For one thing, he *wouldn't* be here. He'd volunteered for duty at the hospital, so that others could be home with their families. And for another thing, Mindy *couldn't* count on him. Not in the way she wanted to. Not in the way she needed. Not in the way she deserved.

"Thanks," he said, turning his attention back to her face again, feeling something inside him tighten a few more notches when he did. "But I'll be working on Christmas Eve. And on Christmas Day, too. Since I don't have a family to spend the holiday with, I figured the least I could do is work and let someone else spend time with theirs."

She nodded her resignation. "I understand. That's awfully nice of you to do that."

Reed almost chuckled at that. His actions hadn't come about because he wanted to do something nice. He'd volunteered to work so that he wouldn't have to be alone, that was all. No sense sitting home by himself when he could be working, taking his mind off the holiday and all its maddening connotations. Being at the hospital over Christmas kept him from dwelling on other things he had no business—or desire—to dwell upon, that was all.

But there was no reason Mindy had to know all that, so he kept his thoughts to himself.

"I should probably get going," he said suddenly.

"So soon?" she asked, her disappointment obvious. "But it's still early."

He did chuckle then. "Mindy, it's nearly one-thirty," he told her, pointing to his wristwatch. "I'd hardly call that early. And you need your rest."

She smiled. "It's early in the morning," she pointed out. "And besides, I'm off tomorrow. I don't have to go to bed yet."

"You know what I meant."

Mindy did know what he meant. And he was right—it was late. She just didn't want him to leave. Because once he was gone, then the evening would be well and truly over. Tonight had been absolutely, without question, the most wonderful, remarkable, magical night of her life. And she didn't want it to end. Not yet.

Not ever.

But she knew it was pointless to try to hang onto something so intangible, something so ephemeral. Something so pointless. All she could do was tuck the memory of this evening into her heart and lock it away for safekeeping. Then, on those nights ahead when she found herself feeling lonely or melancholy, she could take out the memory of tonight and enjoy it all over again.

And she was quite certain that she would do that very thing in the long nights to come. Many, many times. Because, somehow, she sensed it would be a long, long time before she met anyone like Reed again. In fact, she doubted that she would *ever* meet anyone like him again. Or, at the very least, anyone who made her feel the way he made her feel.

"Oh, all right," she said, straightening. "But let me get some of these cookies wrapped up for you before you go."

Hastily, she gathered up an assortment of each kind for him, then rearranged a few containers until there was a hefty collection and variety in one of them for Reed to take to the hospital with him. And all the while she worked, she felt his eyes on her, watching her, considering her, appraising her.

Wanting her?

No, surely he wouldn't be doing that, she answered herself quickly. Even if she did recall now that some of the looks he'd sent her way that night had been positively...voracious. Scandalous. Incandescent.

Oh, boy. It was really getting hot in here.

Mindy swallowed hard, trying not to drop the cookie that threatened to leap out of her hand at the realization of just how aware of Reed she'd been all evening. Of how aware of him she continued to be. He really had been looking at her funny all night, she thought. And they really had shared some conversation that had gone way beyond casual. Something had shifted between them in the last several hours, but she couldn't quite say what. There was just...something... It was just... different... That was all.

And she wanted more than anything in the world to explore

that something more fully, to find out just how, exactly, it *was* different between them.

"Here you go," she said as she snapped shut the lid on one of the medium-sized containers. "That should do you for a few days, anyway. I'll make some more this week. Gotta have some for Santa, after all."

When she glanced up, she saw that Reed was looking at her in that strangely hungry way again, and a similar, almost desperate, need surged up from somewhere deep inside her in response to it. For one long moment, they only stared at each other in silence, their gazes never faltering, their positions never shifting. Mindy's heartbeat escalated with every passing second. Heat surrounded her. All of her senses went on alert. Her awareness of him—of herself—multiplied by thousands.

And suddenly, the only thing in the world she wanted was Reed.

She didn't care what the circumstances were, didn't care how long or how completely she had him. She only knew she needed him in a way she'd never needed anyone or anything before. And somehow, she sensed that he needed her in exactly the same way. For however long. Under whatever circumstances. Even if only for one night. Did she dare? she asked herself. Could she possibly? Then again, was it even up to her at all?

"Reed?" she said breathlessly, her voice scarcely a whisper. "I—is something wrong?"

He shook his head, slowly, certainly, but never once let his attention on her slip. "No. Nothing. Just…"

"What?" she demanded, barely recognizing the husky timbre her own voice had taken on.

He shook his head again, more slowly, more certainly. "You are just so beautiful, Mindy. So…"

As if of their own volition, her lips parted in surprise, and a small sound of surprise escaped her. A wild heat raced through her at the look in his eyes, and she realized suddenly that he did indeed want her. Maybe even as much as she wanted him. But all she could do was stand there, wanting him, hoping he would see how very much. Hoping more that he would act upon it, because she wasn't sure she could find the courage to do that herself.

Reed must have realized then what he'd done, because his cheeks turned ruddy and he quickly looked away. "I'm sorry," he mumbled. "I shouldn't have said that."

"Yes, you should."

Mindy was surprised by her audacity in responding as she had but she couldn't help herself. She'd seen him withdrawing, slipping away from her, and she wanted to pull him back, however she could. She wasn't sure why. It just seemed very important suddenly that he not go away. That they confront whatever it was hanging between them. Now. That they do something—even if it turned out to be the wrong thing—to keep from losing it forever.

"You should always say what's on your mind," she told him, amazed at the steadiness she heard in her voice, when steady was the last thing she felt. "Otherwise," she added, "you might miss a really important opportunity."

He said nothing for a moment, only considered her in silence. Then, very quietly, he asked, "What kind of opportunity?"

She smiled, striving for a lightness she was nowhere close to feeling. "Well, see, that's the kicker. You just never know until it presents itself."

Before she lost her nerve, and without questioning her motives—there would be time enough for that later—Mindy moved from behind the counter that separated them, approaching Reed with slow, measured, and not a little nervous, strides. He watched as she came, saying not a word to stop her, nor to encourage her. She halted when there was still a good foot of space between them, hesitated for a breath of a second, then extended her hand toward him.

But instead of touching him, which was what she really wanted to do, she reached into the breast pocket of his jacket and withdrew the sprig of mistletoe he'd tucked there earlier, after disarming Seth. Then, with a smile she hoped was seductive—but which was probably really pretty scared—she held it above his head. And then, before she had a chance to second-guess herself, she leaned forward and brushed a chaste, though not a quick, kiss across his cheek.

His skin was warm and rough, redolent of something spicy, clean and utterly masculine. And he tasted... Oh...so sweet. Mindy felt herself falling forward, forward, forward, until nothing in the world could halt her descent. Nothing except Reed.

And he did.

Halt her.

By pulling her into his arms.

He groaned as he did so, a lusty, ravenous sound that seemed to come from the deepest part of his soul. Gently, tentatively, he reached for her, tugging her into his lap, clutching her to himself as if he had just unearthed a treasure he'd spent his entire life seeking. For one long moment, he gazed down at her face, and she saw so many emotions warring within the dark depths of his eyes. Then, as if he were no more willing to question his actions than Mindy was, he slowly, oh so slowly, lowered his head to hers and covered her mouth with his.

Fire shot through her at the contact. And with it came an absolute certainty that what they were doing, however it had come about, was utterly and truly right. She wasn't sure how she knew that, but there it was all the same. No matter what happened after this, she thought, this was right. This was good. This was what was meant to be. Mindy didn't think about what would come later. She only thought about now. Reed was a gift, she realized. And she had received so few of those in her life. She wasn't about to reject this one now.

So, eagerly, she looped her arms around his neck and pushed herself more intimately against him, dropping the sprig of mistletoe to the floor, forgotten, so that she could tangle her fingers in the dark silk of his hair. Reed groaned again at the press of her body along his, intensifying the kiss as he splayed one hand open over her back to push her closer still.

With his other hand, he reached for the clip that bound her hair, deftly freeing her blond curls with one swift gesture. Then he wove his fingers through the tumble of curls, cupping his hand at the base of her skull, tipping her head back and to the side so that he could plunder her more completely.

Mindy went limp as his tongue filled her mouth, tangling with hers, tasting her to what felt like the depths of her soul. For long moments, she could do little more than grip the soft fabric of his jacket, challenging him over possession of that kiss. But she surrendered when she felt the hand he had tangled in her hair dipping lower, cupping her cheek, her jaw, skimming along the column of her throat before idly tracing the line of her collarbone. And then he skimmed his fingers lower still, running the backs of his knuckles across the heated, sensitive flesh of her upper breasts where they surged up from the too-tight dress she wore.

"Oh," Mindy cried softly at the brief skin-to-skin contact. "Oh, Reed... Oh, yes... Oh, please..."

Obviously more than willing to comply, he ducked his head to the side of her throat, dragging damp, openmouthed kisses along her neck as he scooped his hand lower to cup her breast firmly in his palm. The sensation that shot through Mindy at the subtle caress was like a wildfire that caught and spread with the rush of a hot summer wind. Because her dress fit so tightly over her pregnancy-swollen breasts, she hadn't bothered to wear a brassiere, and now only a thin layer of soft velvet lay between her and Reed's restless fingers.

And then she felt even that small barrier slip away, when the hand on her back tugged free the zipper behind her. With one easy gesture, Reed pushed her dress down over her shoulders, baring her breasts to the cool night air and the hot onslaught of his hands and mouth. She gasped as he filled both hands with her ripe flesh, running his thumbs over the turgid peaks, palming her, pillaging her, possessing her. And then suddenly his mouth was on her, too, consuming her, sucking hard at her nipples, laving her with the flat of his tongue, taunting her with its tip. He held her fast in one hand as he devoured her, over and over and over again, then switched his attentions to the other side.

Mindy's breath came rapidly, raggedly, until she began to grow dizzy from the rush of heat racing through her entire system. Her eyes fluttered closed as she wove her fingers tightly in his hair and held him close, fearful that he might try to abandon her when she was at her most needy. For a long time, they clung to each other that way, until she thought she would go mad with wanting him. Then, as if he sensed her restlessness, Reed suddenly returned his mouth to hers, kissing her soundly as he lifted her into his arms and stood.

She was barely aware of their movement as he carried her toward his bedroom, but within moments, she lay beneath him on his king-size bed, her dress bunched down around her waist, his jacket and necktie neglected on the floor. Feverishly, she worked at his buttons as he tugged her pantyhose down her legs, then she pushed his shirt from his shoulders as he went to work on the fastening of his trousers.

She watched in silence as he stood to undress, the long rectangle of white spilling through the door offering the only light for the room. She told herself she preferred it that way, because anything brighter would only serve to illuminate whatever insanity had overcome them both. She tried not to think about what was happening, tried only to feel, to respond, to enjoy. And although there were so many things she wanted to say, so many things she wanted to tell Reed, she feared that the simple act of speaking would scatter the fantasy forever, would ruin this brief, however temporary, chance she had for happiness.

At the very back of her brain, a hazy warning buzzed softly, telling her that they were moving too fast, that it was too soon for them to come together this way, that she was risking far too much by allowing this to happen. But Mindy ignored it, squelched it, pretended she hadn't heard. Instead, she opened her arms to Reed in silent invitation.

When he joined her on the bed again, he stretched out alongside her, the heat from his naked body surrounding her, enveloping her in a warm, welcoming embrace. Mindy, too, had shed the rest of her clothing and she turned to him as naked and as vulnerable as he. But when she moved toward him, against him, she inevitably led with her softly swollen belly, something that only reminded them both of her condition.

That's it then, she thought. Reed would come to his senses now, would remember that she was damaged goods, that her future was completely uncertain, that there was no way this would ever work out between them, because there was a third party—that wasn't his—to contend with. And at the reminder of that, naturally, he would flee. Hastily. In horror. Forever.

But instead of turning away in distaste, as she had been so certain he would do, Reed opened his hand gently over the curve of her tummy, palming the taut mound softly once, twice, three times.

"This is so amazing," he said, his voice touched with reverence.

"Yes," she agreed softly. "It is." She smiled, but she said nothing more, still overwhelmed by the miracle of it all herself.

He opened his mouth, as if he were going to say something else, then closed it again and turned his gaze to her face. But even as he focused his attention there, his fingers strummed softly, idly over her womb, as if it were the most natural thing in the world for him to do.

"Are you sure this is what you want?" he asked. "To make love, I mean?"

She covered his hand with hers and nodded. "I'm sure."

"Even though I can't make any promises to you?" he asked, averting his eyes again to watch the way their fingers wove together over her belly.

Not trusting her voice now, she only nodded.

"Even though this may be a huge mistake?" he asked further.

Although she was confident that what they were doing was

in no way a mistake, regardless of the outcome, again, Mindy only nodded silently.

For a moment, Reed didn't respond, neither verbally nor with any kind of gesture. He only lay on his side next to her, his hand cupped gently over her tummy, his chest rising and falling in an irregular rhythm that mirrored her own. Then slowly, very slowly, he freed his fingers from hers and scooted his hand forward, curving his fingers over her hip, pushing his palm down to her thigh. And then, expertly, easily, he nudged her onto her back, tucking his hand between her legs to gently urge them apart.

She fell back willingly onto the bed, opening to him, prepared for the touch of his fingertips against her dewy folds, eagerly awaiting that tender exploration. What she wasn't expecting, however—and what she wasn't prepared for—was the brush of his mouth there instead. She gasped when she realized his intention and started to cry out an objection. Sam had never…no one had ever…

When she felt the soft butterfly flutter of his tongue against that most sensitive part of her, her entire body went lax. Never before had she experienced the wild sizzle of sensation that rocked her at such an intimate contact. Never before had she understood what it was that truly made a woman feel like a woman. Now she knew. As Reed increased his ministrations, as he buried his head between her legs, as he clutched her bottom in both hands to lift her higher, more fully against his mouth, as he pleasured her with his tongue, his lips, his hot breath, Mindy realized how much more there was between a man and a woman than she had ever known.

Higher and higher he carried her with his delicious loving, until she thought she would come undone with the sensations uncurling inside her. And then she did come undone, as a burst of something explosive and hot both filled her and emptied her in one long rush.

For a moment, she could only lay unmoving as she gasped for breath, certain that she would never again experience such an overriding, overwhelming joy no matter how long she lived. What Reed had done, what he'd made her feel… It was like nothing else could ever be. *He* was like no one else would ever be.

And there would be no one else after him. Of that, Mindy was suddenly very certain. Battling the dark, needful fog that threatened to usurp her, she tried to tell him that. But before she had the chance, he was rolling onto his back beside her, pulling her atop and astride him.

"Ride me," he said as he gripped her hips fiercely in both hands. "It'll be easier for you that way."

"B-but what about you?" she asked, only half-coherent to what he was telling her. Still feeling dizzy and muddled, she strove to steady herself, curling her fingers into the dark, springy hair scattered across his chest and torso. Beneath her fingertips, she felt the gentle ripple of muscle and sinew, heat and hard flesh, and a rapid-fire heartbeat running as rampant as her own.

He smiled, a sexy, satisfied smile that fed the flames licking at her heart. Then he reached up and filled both hands with her breasts, squeezing her nipples between the deep V's of his index and middle fingers. "Oh, believe me…this way is just fine with me." He rubbed his hands over her sensitive flesh, then murmured, "C'mon, Mindy. Ride me."

His voice was rough, rich with his need, and she was helpless not to obey him. She pushed herself up on her knees and moved backward, until she felt the hard length of him—oh, there was so much of him—nudging at the sensitive cleft of her bottom. Somehow she found the strength to raise herself higher still, and move back a bit more, until the plump head of his shaft pressed against her damp, heated core. Slowly, very slowly, she began to lower herself onto him, feeling stretched and filled as he entered her. He closed his eyes and groaned loud and long as she took him inside her, and she echoed the sound with every long inch of his penetration.

He seemed to fill her entire body when she finally settled herself completely against him, so acute, so exquisite, was his possession of her, and hers of him. For a moment, she only sat still, letting her body adjust to his invasion, letting his body adjust to her conquest.

And then, very slowly, she began to move. Up she rode him, then down, the easy friction of their slick bodies doubling their heat, doubling their pleasure, doubling their fire. Up again, slowly, slowly, then down, down, oh…down again. Little by little, Mindy increased the pace, until both seemed ready to explode. Somehow, Reed felt larger with every thrust, and somehow, Mindy opened more to accommodate him.

And then, when he could obviously tolerate no more of her slow possession, Reed picked up the pace himself, launching himself into her, bucking up to meet her every time she moved down. He gripped her hips hard in both fists and held her still, pummeling her from below until she was almost insensate. And just when she thought she would go spiraling out into the cosmos, he arched one final time against her, muttering something feral and primitive as he spilled himself deep inside her.

And then suddenly, Mindy was on her back and Reed was kneeling between her legs. With each hand, he encircled one of her ankles, and he spread her wide for one final thrust, to empty himself entirely inside her. Her own climax came then, hurtling her out into a bright kaleidoscope of color and sensation, a place from which she hoped to never return. The last thing she saw before closing her eyes was Reed collapsing beside her. The last thing she felt was his warm, damp breath against her naked breasts. And the last thing she heard was the sound of his heartbeat, mirroring exactly the rhythm of her own.

Ten

What had he done? Oh, God, what had he done?

Reed lay on his side next to Mindy in the big king-size bed he'd never planned on sharing with anyone, ever, wondering where, exactly, he'd gone wrong the night before. Thankfully, she still slept soundly, something that offered him a few precious moments with which he could berate himself in peace. But she was turned on her side toward him, so that even in the dusky light of early dawn that sneaked through the closed window blinds, he could look upon her face.

It was rather a mixed blessing at the moment.

Although Reed would have sworn it was impossible, she was more beautiful this morning than she had been last night. A spill of pale gold curls tumbled lazily over her forehead, and he fought the urge to reach out and push them lovingly back. Her cheeks were pink and glowing, her mouth curved into a soft, contented little smile, and he had to force himself not to lean down and brush his own lips over every sweet inch of her face.

The covers had dipped low while she slept and were bunched around her waist, but she had folded one arm over her breasts, her open palm settled against the bedsheet before her. In spite of her position and the chill air in the room, Reed could see the flush of last night's heat still staining the ivory skin above her breasts, and something inside him grew warm in response with wanting her.

Which was the last thing he needed right now. The clock on the opposite nightstand read 6:27, and he was due at the hospital at 7:30. There was no way he'd have time to drive all the way to Ardmore and back, no way he'd be able to shower and change at home this morning. He would have to do that here, at his temporary residence—which oddly enough, for some reason, suddenly felt anything *but* temporary, and suddenly felt more like home than home did.

He shook the strange impression off as quickly as it formed in his muddled brain. Instead, he tried to focus on the gargantuan obstacle he had facing him at the moment—that in the process of readying himself for work here, he would almost certainly wake Mindy. And the last thing he wanted or needed right now was to have to face her and to confront what had happened last night.

Because the problem was he just didn't know what the hell *had* happened last night. One minute, he'd been telling Mindy he had to leave—and he'd had every intention of doing so— and the next, he'd been filling his mouth with her lush heat. He got hard all over again with the simple memory of how she'd responded to him, how she'd tasted, how she'd sounded, how she'd felt as she came apart in his arms.

Oh, man...

He'd never lost control like that before, had never let his impulses override his good sense. Especially not where a woman was concerned. Especially not where a pregnant woman was concerned. Especially not where a pregnant woman who deserved so much more than he could give her was concerned. And he still couldn't quite recall what had commanded him to make such a huge leap forward in his relationship with Mindy, without so much as a "Mother, may I?"

The phrasing of that last thought made him groan inwardly. She was a mother-to-be, her reminded himself again ruthlessly. A woman whose pregnancy—by another man, no less—was well and truly showing. Yet he'd just had the most intense, most delirious, most satisfying sex of his entire life with her.

How could that be? he wondered. Not only should he have been put off sexually by the realization that she was pregnant with another man's child, but the knowledge of her condition—and the fact that her future was completely up in the air right now—should have offered him all the rationale he needed to avoid the very entanglement he'd just willingly fallen into.

But instead of being repelling, the sight of her ripe, naked body, full and lush to nurture her unborn child, had turned Reed on faster than he'd ever been turned on in his life. And the knowledge that she was going to have a baby, even if it wasn't his, had stirred an intense emotional response inside him that, coupled with his need for her physically, had simply been too much for him to comprehend, too much for him to resist.

Why? he asked himself again. Why? Why? Why?

But instead of answers, he only received more questions in response. How could this have happened? And what was he going to do about it? How could he make Mindy understand, after what the two of them had just shared, that he had to leave this morning, and, quite frankly, he wasn't sure when he'd be back? That he might *never* be back? Not emotionally, at any rate, not the way he was last night.

Certainly he wouldn't abandon her—he'd be around to make sure she had what she needed here at the condo for as long as it took her to get back on her feet. And he'd be there for her even after she found a place to live, if she'd allow him that. But there was no way they could possibly repeat what had happened last night. Because to do so would... It would...

Well, it would just be disruptive, that was all, to both their lives. And Reed didn't need or want a disruption in his life. Nor did Mindy need one in hers.

But how could he explain all that to her, when he couldn't quite understand it himself?

He bit back a groan at all the troubling, mangled thoughts that were tumbling about in his brain. He really did have to get going if he was going to make it to the hospital on time. He had to rush. He had to flee. He had to escape. He had to run like hell away from here and figure out what to do about the mess he'd made of things.

Unfortunately, it didn't look as if he would be given any sort of reprieve, because there was no way he could avoid waking Mindy before he left. That gave him maybe fifteen minutes in the shower to figure out what he was going to say to her. Fifteen minutes to figure out what the hell had happened in the first place. Fifteen minutes to understand the bizarre, incomprehensible workings of his own brain.

In spite of his realization that a confrontation was unavoidable, Reed sought to postpone it for as long as he could by easing himself out of bed as slowly as possible. He held his breath and watched her closely with every move he made, and continued to study her intently as he crept backward, toward the adjoining bathroom. But she never so much as altered her breathing pattern, only continued to sleep in blissful ignorance of the situation.

Exhaling a sigh of relief himself, Reed closed the door, then, as an afterthought, and with only a moment's hesitation, he locked it. Surely in the time it took him to shower and shave, he'd figure out where the scales had tipped so precariously the night before. He'd figure out what to say to Mindy to explain things and make them right again. He'd figure out just what that jumble of strange feelings inside him meant.

Surely he would. Surely.

Unfortunately, twenty-five minutes later, Reed realized that fifteen minutes—or even twenty-five minutes, for that matter—was in no way enough time for a person to figure out the workings of capricious fate or a muddled brain. Because even after he'd finished shaving and slipped into a dark-blue, terry cloth bathrobe he was no closer to understanding his predicament than he'd been upon waking. He still had no idea how to explain his actions—or his feelings—to Mindy. Or to himself. He still had no idea how to rectify the situation. And he still had no idea why his emotions were in such a tumultuous uproar.

It was only sex, he tried to tell himself. That was all. What was the big deal? He'd had sex before, and he'd dealt with the morning-after thing with no trouble at all, usually just by having more sex. He was a grown man, and Mindy was a grown woman. There was no reason why they couldn't just sit down and calmly discuss what had happened last night and what it meant for them—or, more precisely, what it *didn't* mean for them—in the future.

Sex, he repeated to himself. That was all it had been. It wasn't the end of the world.

Inhaling a deep breath that he assured himself was *not* shaky, Reed opened the bathroom door and exited. And he steeled himself in preparation of finding Mindy on the other side, either sitting up in bed waiting for him or seated in the kitchen with a cup of coffee, waiting for him, or perched on the sofa, reading the paper—waiting for him.

But she wasn't in bed. She wasn't in the kitchen. She wasn't in the living room, either. Nor was she on the balcony—not surprising, seeing as how it was probably only about twenty degrees outside—nor was she in the spare bedroom, nor in the alcove off the kitchen. She wasn't in any of the closets—yes, he checked, which just went to show how very befuddled his brain was this morning—nor was she in any of the kitchen cabinets.

In fact, there was no sign of Mindy anywhere. When Reed opened the front door to glance down the hallway outside, he saw nothing but the *Philadelphia Inquirer* folded neatly on the floor in front of the apartment across the hall. Certainly there was no Mindy. Nor was there any sign that she had ever existed at all. He closed the door thoughtfully behind him as he went back inside, halfway wondering if he had simply dreamed everything that had happened the last two weeks. If so, it had been some dream. One that made him want to go right back to bed for a second helping.

Where could she be? he asked himself. Why would she have just left without a word? And where had she gone? It hadn't been more than a half hour since he'd awakened, so she didn't have time to go far. Still, her disappearance made no sense at all.

Reed sighed heavily again and glanced at the clock in the kitchen. He was due in surgery early this morning, so there was no way he could take time out to search for the mysterious vanishing Mindy. And, truth be told, he couldn't deny the relief that wound through him at the knowledge that she had offered him this reprieve.

Well, he was sort of relieved at any rate. Kind of. In a way. Wasn't he? Sure, he was. That had to be relief winding through him. Even if, suddenly, it did feel a little like regret.

But of course he would have regrets, he told himself as he headed for his bedroom to dress. Last night had been, at best, a mistake, at worst, a total disaster. Naturally, he'd feel regretful. Funny thing was, though, he had a sneaking suspicion that what had happened between him and Mindy last night *wasn't* what he was regretting right now.

"You're an idiot, Atchison," he muttered aloud to himself. Hell, he didn't even know what he was feeling this morning. And something told him the day was only going to get worse from here.

With another glance at the clock on the nightstand, he opened the closet door, content to make do with one of the suits he left here for exactly this purpose. And he tried not to think about how, suddenly, nothing in the condo—or his life— felt quite right.

In the coffee shop across the street from Reed's condo, Mindy snuggled deeper into her coat at a table by the window, and tried to look like a woman whose world hadn't just come tumbling down around her. She nursed a cup of decaf and picked at a cinnamon-raisin bagel, wishing he would hurry up and leave so she could go back home and take a shower. Then a rapid thread of heat unwound inside her at what she had just thought. *Home.* She considered Reed's condo to be home now.

Great. This was all she needed.

"You're an idiot, Mindy," she mumbled under her breath. "A first-class, see-exhibit-A idiot."

When she'd awakened that morning, it had been to the sound of Reed taking a shower in the room next door, and for one brief, joyful moment, she had felt utterly, exquisitely *right.* In the half-consciousness of waking, she had recalled bits and pieces of the night that had passed, had remembered the soft words she and Reed had exchanged, had relived the gentle touches, the intimate joining of their bodies, the even more intimate mingling of their souls. And for just a moment, everything in her world had just seemed...

Perfect.

Then wakefulness had claimed her. Her brain had cleared and comprehension had descended, and the full implication of what the two of them had done had come crashing down around her. And the first thought that had shot through her mind was escape. She hadn't wanted to face Reed yet, hadn't wanted to see how he would react. She was chicken—she admitted that without hesitation. But her feelings for him were simply too new, too fragile, too uncertain for her to share them just yet. Had Reed somehow detected how she felt about him, he might very well—unwittingly, of course—crush those feelings underfoot.

Somewhere over the last two weeks—even before last night—she had fallen in love with him. There was no question in her mind about that. And she had no idea what she was going to do about it.

Did he return the feeling? Could he possibly feel for her the same way she felt for him? Was there any chance at all that what had happened last night had come about as a mutual response to the same emotion? Had they turned to each other because they loved and needed each other? Or was it only because they needed each other in a more superficial sense? Was it only because they were lonely? Because they missed the simple presence of another warm body in their lives?

Of course, Mindy knew the answer to those questions where she was concerned. What had happened between her and Reed last night had come about because of her love for him. Because she needed him in the most basic, most elemental way. Because she couldn't imagine her life ahead without him. But everything suddenly seemed so complicated. They'd known each other such a short time. They came from two entirely different worlds. She was carrying a baby who would be entering the world in a matter of months. A baby that wasn't his.

Could Reed possibly overlook all those things to see his way clear to his feelings for her? And just what were his feelings for her anyway? Certainly she knew he cared for her. No one could have made love the way they had without there being some kind of affection on both parties' parts. But affection didn't necessarily lead to a forever-after, till-death-do-us-part kind of love. And affection wasn't always permanent.

Reed was nearing forty yet he'd never married, she reminded herself. From what she could tell, he'd never even come close. There must be a reason for that. He was too kind and decent and attractive a man to have remained single unless that was exactly how he wanted to spend his life. And heaven knew if that was the case, there was little chance he'd want to take on a package deal like Mindy and her unborn child. Hey, hadn't she told him often enough that she wasn't his responsibility?

Her breath caught as the door to his building opened and he strode through it. Even from across the street, he looked every bit as handsome as he did up close, dressed in a dark suit and darker overcoat that flapped open in the cold morning breeze.

Some doctor, she thought with a sad smile. Didn't even have enough sense to button himself up when it was cold outside. The wind caught and flirted with his hair, and he shoved a gloved hand through the black tresses to keep them out of his eyes. Then he turned toward the parking lot and made his way to his car, a sleek silver Jaguar that only reminded Mindy how very different the two of them were. She'd be taking the bus to work today.

Only when he had turned out of the parking lot and into the street did she release a breath she'd been unaware of holding. And only when he was fully out of sight did she allow herself to consider her options. For now, she thought, she would just try to take it a little at a time. She was due at work in a few hours so she'd spend the morning as she usually did, preparing for that. Then, of course, the afternoon would be filled with her shift at the diner. She got off after the dinner rush, so she'd go home after that.

But to what? she asked herself. What would be waiting for her upon her return to Reed's condo tonight? Would there be anything at all?

That was the big question, Mindy thought. She only wished she had an answer to go with it. Unfortunately, Reed was the only one who could provide it. And as well as she'd come to know him over the last two weeks—and over the last night— she had no idea what his answer would be.

"Forget about it. There's no point to it. It's not going to happen. Not ever."

Reed shook his head at Seth as he muttered those words with as much conviction as he could muster—even if he couldn't quite manage to *feel* much conviction at all. He wasn't sure how it had happened but over a late lunch—someplace *other* than Evie's Diner—Reed had spilled his guts to Seth about what had happened the night before. Or, at least, he'd let slip the fact that he and Mindy had slept together. He hadn't, however, been able to bring himself to discuss at length the feelings and uncertainties that went along with the physical aspect of their joining.

Seth was his best friend, to be sure, but there were some things a man didn't discuss, even with his best friend. Not first, anyway. And somehow, talking to Seth about his feelings for Mindy—whatever the hell they were—before he'd broached the subject with her, just seemed like a betrayal for some reason. At any rate, Reed hadn't felt comfortable telling Seth how he felt—or didn't feel, or whatever the hell was going on inside him. Which was just as well. Because clearly, Reed still wasn't sure just how he felt at all.

That hadn't kept Seth from uttering his opinion on the subject however. And, as always, Seth's opinion was just about the dumbest damned thing Reed had ever heard in his life.

"What do you mean there's no point to it?" Seth retorted. "You and Mindy are great together. I think you ought to marry her. It would be the perfect arrangement for both of you."

Marry her? Reed repeated to himself. *Marry* her? Marry Mindy? Why would he do a thing like that to her? He *liked* Mindy. He wouldn't for a minute wish something on her like marriage to him.

"And just how the hell do you figure it would be a perfect arrangement?" Reed demanded of Seth, trying to ignore the swirl of something hot, heedless and hopeful that welled up inside him at hearing his friend's suggestion. It was a dumb idea, he told himself again. Dumb. Really dumb.

"Hey, Mindy needs a place to stay and a father for her baby," Seth pointed out. "And you need somebody to make a human being out of you. It's perfect," he reiterated dryly. "You each have something the other needs. You have a home, and she has a heart."

Reed grimaced at Seth's supposedly lighthearted take on the matter. He should have known his friend couldn't be serious about this. "Mindy and I just met two weeks ago," he reminded the other man. "That's not long enough for two people to know each other before deciding to get married. You're being ridiculous.''

Not to mention terrifying, Reed added to himself.

He eyed his friend thoughtfully. ''You, after all, have dated every woman on the planet and still haven't found anyone to share your life with beyond a casual fling.''

Seth shrugged carelessly, but there was something about the gesture that seemed anything but careless. ''I haven't dated quite *every* woman,'' he said. And he said it in a way that made Reed suspect there was one woman in particular Seth was thinking about—one he maybe thought about pretty often. ''Besides,'' he added quickly, ''there's a lot to be said for casual flings. I, myself, rather *like* casual flings. But then, we weren't talking about me, were we? We were talking about you.''

More's the pity, Reed thought.

''You and Mindy,'' Seth clarified. As if that particular topic needed any clarification. ''You and Mindy and what you plan to do about this significant new development in your relationship.''

''She and I don't have a relationship,'' Reed was quick to counter. ''That's the whole point.''

Seth uttered a rude sound of disbelief. ''Please,'' he said. ''Don't even try to delude yourself in that respect. All you'll do is wind up embarrassing yourself.''

''I *don't* have a relationship with her,'' he insisted.

''Uh-huh. Right. And Arnold Schwarzenegger sleeps in a pink bra and tutu every night.''

Reed glared at his friend. ''Yeah, well, to each his own, I guess.''

Seth shook his head with obvious disappointment. ''If I live to be a hundred I'll never understand what motivates you,'' he said. ''You have something—someone—right there for the taking that will make you happy, but you just won't let yourself reach out and claim it.''

''That's because it's not mine for the claiming,'' Reed said softly.

Seth eyed him thoughtfully for a moment. "I think that's really up to Mindy to decide, don't you?"

Reed shook his head. "Right now, her life is in a complete uproar. Six months ago she was in an entirely different place than she is right now. In that short space of time, she's become pregnant, she's lost her husband, she's lost her home. How the hell can she trust her emotions after all that? There's nothing certain for her right now or in her future. She has no idea what she wants or needs."

"Doesn't she?"

"Of course not."

"I reiterate, Reed. I think that's up to Mindy—not you—to decide."

Reed inhaled deeply, ready to refute his friend's analysis of the situation with one easy, dismissive point. Unfortunately, he couldn't quite put his finger on what that point was.

"Talk to her, Reed," Seth said. "That's all you have to do."

"You make it sound so simple."

"That's because it is simple."

This time Reed was the one to expel an incredulous sound. "You've got to be kidding. Simple is the last thing this situation is. Besides, Mindy and I aren't the only ones at stake here."

"Oh, no?"

Reed shook his head. "No. There's the future of her baby to think about. And as a mother, she's obligated to do what's best for her baby."

"And what would be best for her baby?" Seth asked.

But Reed said nothing, afraid to even think about that.

"A father," Seth immediately answered his own question. "Her baby needs a father who will love him or her, nurture him or her and care for him or her. As devotedly as his or her mother will."

"And that's exactly the problem," Reed told him, a strange melancholy unwinding in his belly as he formed the words.

But clearly, Seth didn't understand. "And that problem would be...?"

Reed hesitated only a moment before saying, "That I'm just not cut out to be a father."

Seth hesitated a moment, too, before speaking. Then, quietly, he asked, "Says who?"

"Says generations of Atchison men before me, that's who. We're not genetically predisposed to be caring, nurturing men."

For a long time, Seth only gazed at him, and Reed had no idea what was going on in the other man's brain. Still, there was obviously something going on. The expression on Seth's face was downright...plotting. Then, suddenly, his features cleared and he glanced up from the table to catch the eye of their server. "Check, please!" he called out.

Reed narrowed his eyes suspiciously. "Where are we going?" he asked.

Seth smiled. "On a sentimental journey."

Reed narrowed his eyes even more suspiciously. "What are you talking about?"

But Seth's smile only grew broader as he reached into his jacket for his wallet. "Reed, my friend," he said as he searched for and plucked down his credit card, "consider this a haunting."

"A haunting?"

Seth nodded, smiling with smug satisfaction. "After I settle up our bill, you and I are going to go have a quick look at Christmas yet-to-come."

"So...do you come here often?" Reed considered the question to be a very good one as he turned to pose it to his friend, considering where the two of them were standing.

"Yeah," Seth told him as he flattened both hands against the window before him, that single, softly uttered word creating a perfect circle of fog on the glass near his mouth. "I try to get up here at least once a week."

Reed returned his gaze to the sight beyond the window,

curious and intrigued by its contents, but also more than a little wary. ''Why?'' he asked.

Seth shrugged. ''Well, for one thing, the nurses on this floor are really, really hot.''

Reed rolled his eyes, but said nothing.

''Well, except for Ed,'' Seth qualified. ''But for another thing,'' he then continued easily, ''coming here reminds me that there are some things in life that go way beyond our comprehension, some things in life that simply supersede all the other stuff that we so foolishly think is important.''

Reed studied the occupants beyond the glass more critically, gradually taking in the dozens of pink-and-blue-striped, flannel-clad bundles. And he tried to see things Seth's way. Truly, he did. But really, all he saw were a bunch of wizened, puckered, sometimes sleeping, frequently squalling babies. And he wondered about what his friend had said earlier, about Christmas yet-to-come.

''I'm afraid you've lost me,'' he said honestly. ''I don't understand what this has to do with anything we've talked about today.''

''Then you're an idiot,'' Seth said succinctly.

Reed arched his eyebrows in affront. ''Excuse me?''

''I said, you're an idiot,'' his friend repeated.

''How do you figure?''

''You just are.''

Without further comment, he rapped softly on the glass with the backs of his knuckles, catching the attention of a nurse standing in the nursery, a lovely, flame-haired woman whose tightly wound braid hung to the center of her back. She was dressed in raspberry-colored scrubs and she smiled when she recognized Seth, then nodded eagerly.

''Come on,'' he told Reed. Then he strode toward a door to their left without even waiting to see what his response would be.

Grumbling under his breath, Reed followed like a well-trained spaniel, though his own pace slowed somewhat when he heard the howling of a score of babies erupt as Seth opened the door. In spite of his misgivings, he followed his friend through the L shape of corridors that ultimately led to the nursery itself, marveling that in all his years at Seton General he'd never set foot on this entire floor. Not surprisingly, Seth immediately struck up a conversation with the redheaded nurse, whose name tag, in addition to bearing brightly colored stickers of Disney characters, proclaimed her to be Zoey Holland-Tate.

"Oh, yeah," she was saying, "we're packed. That full moon two nights ago really pushed us to the limit. Go ahead and have a look around," she added with a smile, thrusting a mask, gloves and scrubs toward Seth, which he immediately handed to Reed.

So Nurse Zoey handed him another set for himself, and Seth routinely donned the garments, indicating that he did, indeed, partake of this activity on a fairly regular basis. Reed, too, put on the necessary accoutrements for newborn observing and when he looked up he saw Seth watching the retreating form of Zoey Holland-Tate, who, if Reed wasn't mistaken, was the wife of Dr. Jonas Tate, one of Seton General's most muckety-muck administrators.

"She is so hot," Seth said reverently under his breath.

Reed nodded, not exactly surprised by his friend's assessment. "She's an older woman, pal. She'd make mincemeat out of you."

"Doesn't matter," Seth said. "She's still hot."

"She's a wife and mother."

"Doesn't matter. She's still hot."

"Her husband, and the father of her children, also happens to be your boss."

Seth turned his attention back to Reed. "Oh, yeah. Matters. I guess. But she's still hot."

Reed wasn't sure, but he thought Seth was still smiling—probably salaciously—behind his mask.

"Come on," his friend said. "Let's find a live one."

As they strode among the clear plastic bassinets that housed all variety of newborn infants, Reed found himself reluctantly warming a bit inside. Even if they were all wizened, puckered and squalling, they were kind of cute. In their own…wrinkled way.

"Ah," Seth said as he came to a halt a few bassinets ahead. "Here we go. Baby girl. Eight pounds, eleven ounces. Three days old. Delivered by C-section. She's going home with her mommy and daddy today."

Without ceremony—or asking permission of anyone, something that made Reed glance about a bit anxiously—Seth reached into the bassinet and tucked the small bundle into his arms. Then he turned carefully toward Reed and said, "Here."

"What?" Reed asked, confused.

Seth extended the tiny baby forward. "Take her."

"What?"

"Take her," his friend repeated. "Hold her a minute."

"Are you nuts?"

"Of course not. Hold her."

"But…but… But that baby belongs to someone," Reed objected.

"Yeah, she does," Seth conceded eagerly. "Isn't it *great?* Somebody gets to take this sweet little thing home today and enjoy her for years to come. They'll watch her learn to crawl and walk, they'll see her first teeth come in, they'll put her on a big, yellow school bus someday and send her off to first grade. There will be years full of birthdays and kittens and gymnastics meets and braces and homecoming dances and heartbreaking rites of passage. And her parents will be there to help her through each and every one of them. And they'll love her more and more with every passing day."

Reed couldn't recall Seth ever being so sentimental and maudlin but he had to grudgingly admit that his friend wore it well.

"When you look at something like this," he said softly, turning his attention to the baby in his arms, "when you think about all that goes into the forming and nurturing of a human being… Well, it just sorta makes everything else in the world seem kinda inconsequential, doesn't it?"

Reed said nothing. Mainly because he had no idea what to say.

"Come on," Seth cajoled gently, looking up at Reed again. "Take her. Hold her. It's okay. We're doctors, man. We know what we're doing."

Reed expelled a soft sound of doubt. "Speak for yourself."

"Cradling a baby is a natural human response," Seth assured him. "It's instinctive."

"Not with men," Reed said.

Seth rolled his eyes. "Of course with men."

"Not with Atchison men."

Seth shook his head, but with the mask on, Reed couldn't quite tell what his friend was thinking. "It's a natural human response with anyone who has half a heart," he stated adamantly. And you, Reed—I think it's time you just admitted it—have a heart. A whole heart. A great, big whole heart. You've just never been given a chance to use it properly." More emphatically, he said, "Take…the…baby. Now."

Without assessing the way his resolve—and his fear—seemed to be dissolving slowly inside him, and with less reluctance than he thought he should feel, Reed reached forward to take the infant. For a moment he wasn't sure how to hold the baby, but Seth clearly knew what he was doing and arranged the tiny creature in Reed's arms so that he felt comfortable enough that he wouldn't drop her. And once that anxiety was gone, the most amazing thing happened.

Reed realized that he kind of liked holding the baby in his arms.

An odd ripple of happiness wound through him as he grew more accustomed to the weight and feel of the infant bundled close to his chest, and he kind of liked that, too. She slept soundly in his arms, one hand freed of her blanket and fisted loosely by her cheek, her mouth a tiny O with her tongue pressed against it. Then she yawned, rather largely, and Reed chuckled at the sight of it. The sound of his quiet laughter woke her, and slowly, her eyes opened a bit. She squinted at him, hard, and he waited for her to howl a protest at being held by a stranger.

But instead of crying, she only opened her eyes a bit wider and stared at him. Stared at him as if she didn't mind being held in his arms at all. In fact, so comfortable was she there that she promptly fell right back to sleep again. But not before her fingers uncurled from her cheek and somehow rewound themselves around his thumb.

And then Reed enjoyed a sensation of warmth and well-being unlike anything he'd ever experienced before, a feeling that there was something out there at work that was infinitely larger and more important than he was himself. It suddenly seemed to him that there was a continuity to, and interconnectedness of, all things, a cyclical nature to life that he'd never really considered before. As if everything in the world had a purpose and a meaning, and all those purposes and meanings were bundled up together into one big opportunity.

As if there were no endings and no beginnings, just repeated chances to do things right, to correct past mistakes—however long it took to do it—so that the future could be lived without regrets. And he kind of liked that idea, too.

He also kind of liked the idea of doing this baby-holding thing on a more regular basis. And he realized that family genetics really had very little in common with family traditions.

Huh. How about that? Who knew?

It wasn't one's DNA that made a person cold or warm, shunning or loving, uncaring or decent, he thought. It was simply a matter of heart. Gee. You'd think a cardiologist would have figured that out by now.

"My, my, my," Seth said softly, and only then did Reed remember that his friend was even there. "Would you just look at the time?"

"Mmm," Reed murmured absently, looking at the baby instead.

"I really do have to get going."

"Mmm."

"I have surgery scheduled in a half hour."

"Mmm."

"But, listen, why don't you just stay here for a little while? Zoey won't mind. And neither will any of the other nurses. They love having me here."

"Mmm."

"Well, except maybe one…"

Once again, Seth's tone of voice caught Reed's attention—however halfheartedly—and he got the feeling his friend was thinking again about someone who commanded a good deal of his attention.

"But she'll come around," Seth stated with what was clearly forced, and feigned, certainty. "I am, after all, irresistible. Dr. Irresistible, in fact. She wants me. I'm—almost—sure of it."

"Mmm, yeah. Sure, Seth. Whatever you say."

When he glanced up at his friend, even Seth's mask couldn't hide his irritation at Reed's remark. "Yeah, well… Anyway. Don't be a stranger, Reed. Come up here whenever you like."

Reed nodded. "Maybe I will."

"Oh, and do talk to Mindy, will ya?"

He nodded again. "Definitely, I will."

"Christmas yet-to-come is all well and good," Seth said, "but there's a lot to be said for Christmas present, too."

"Certainly more than there is to be said for Christmas past," Reed muttered to himself. But then, there was no reason to dwell on those, he thought. Not when there were so many Christmases in the future waiting with his family.

"Have a good one, Reed," Seth said as he left the nursery.

Reed snuggled the little baby closer for a moment before saying to his friend's retreating back, "Oh, I will, Seth. I most certainly will."

Eleven

Mindy lay alone in the big bed she'd shared with Reed twenty-four hours earlier—had it really only been last night that they turned to each other with such need?—and stared at the clock on the nightstand. Just shy of ten-thirty, and there was still no sign of him. Not unless she counted the clothes he'd worn yesterday, which had been folded neatly on the chair by the dresser—and which she hadn't had the heart to move, just in case it was the last she ever saw of him. Not unless she counted the faint scent of him that still clung to the sheets, taunting her with memories of their loving. Not unless she counted the way he lingered so vividly in her thoughts. Except for all those intangible reminders of Reed, she was well and truly alone.

Was this the way she was destined to feel for the rest of her life? she wondered.

She turned restlessly onto her side and gazed at the telephone, for all the good that would do. Not only had it not rung once since she'd been home, but earlier, after pushing aside any semblance of pride she had left, she'd telephoned Reed's house in Ardmore, only to have the line ring and ring and ring at the other end without being answered by anyone—either human or mechanical. She'd called the hospital, too, and had been told that Dr. Atchison had signed out hours ago, at the end of his regular shift. He'd never shown up at Evie's—for lunch *or* dinner, because Mindy had stayed around after her shift to see if he would. And now, for the life of her, she couldn't think of anyplace else he might be.

Except maybe *gone*.

For good? She wished she knew. Naturally, she'd have to see him again at some point—she was, after all, squatting on his property. But just what would the terms of that meeting be? she wondered. Would he pretend nothing had ever happened? Would he be angry? Would he be disappointed? Would he have any kind of reaction at all?

She sighed heavily as she considered the possibilities, none of which seemed particularly appealing. If he were happy about what the two of them had shared last night, he would have hurried home from work. Or he would have come into the diner to see her. He would, at the very least, have called her, to tell her he was thinking about her, that he'd been transformed by their lovemaking, that he would love her forever and ever and ever. One thing he *wouldn't* do was stay away. Yet that was precisely what he'd done.

And here, she'd been hoping she might be getting something really nice for Christmas this year.

She closed her eyes and tried to will herself to sleep, knowing that particular endeavor was going to be pretty much pointless. Still, she must have managed to doze some, because the next thing she knew she was opening her eyes, and the clock on the nightstand indicated it was just shy of midnight. And naturally, in her state of semi-consciousness, the first thought that flitted through her head was, *Where's Reed?*

As if cued by the silent question, a soft sound rose from the other side of the bedroom door, one that had Mindy shooting straight up in bed, fully awake. For a moment, she didn't move a muscle, only cocked her head to the side to see if she heard the sound again. It was muffled, kind of distant, but it sounded a lot like…

Jingle bells?

Not the song "Jingle Bells" but actual jingle bells. Like the ones attached to Santa's sleigh. But Santa wasn't due to appear for another week, she reminded herself. So if there were jingle bells out there now, it could only mean one of two things. Either there was a burglar in the condo who had a really sick sense of humor or else Reed had finally decided to come home.

A soft smile curled her lips. Ever the optimist, Mindy expected that the latter was true.

As quietly as she could, she shoved the covers away and stood, tugging her flannel jammies—the blue ones that were decorated with big white snowflakes—into place as best she could. She pushed her hair back from her face, deciding not to worry right now that it was doubtless a riot of tangled, uncooperative curls. Instead, she tiptoed to the bedroom door and very, very quietly turned the knob and pulled it open a few inches to look beyond.

The view afforded her was only a partial one of the living room, but she definitely heard the sound of someone moving around out there. And every so often, that soft, merry jingle of bells that had her smiling more broadly. Just what was he up to out there?

Her question received an immediate answer when Reed finally came into view. At least, she thought it was Reed. It certainly *looked* like Reed—same height, same build, same dark hair. But, gosh, she'd never seen him dressed quite *that* way before…

The red Santa suit was clearly a few sizes too big for him, because it was bunched at the waist under a huge black patent leather belt. The coat, too, bagged out around its binding. Upon closer inspection—no easy feat, considering the fact that there was barely any light out there, and what was out there seemed to be…twinkling?—she noted that the Santa suit had definitely seen better days, because it appeared to have a patch on one elbow and a couple of bare spots on the fake fur.

Still, Mindy certainly wasn't going to call Santa on a lack of sartorial splendor. The last thing she needed was a lump of coal in her stocking. And hey, even sartorially challenged, Santa was one hunka hunka burnin' love.

Her thoughts must have given her away, because he glanced up then and caught her spying on him. But instead of disappearing into a puff of magic smoke, as any self-respecting Santa would do, he smiled at her.

"Merry Christmas, Mindy," he said softly.

Surely she was dreaming, she thought. Surely she had nodded off completely as she waited for Reed to come home and what she was seeing now was nothing more than a hope-engendered, sugarplum-inspired fantasy playing itself out in her head. Because the Reed Atchison she knew and loved would never, ever, not in a million billion years dress up like—

Wait a minute, she stopped herself. The Reed she knew and loved would dress up like Santa in a heartbeat. The Reed Atchison *Reed* had thought he was wouldn't. But the one she knew him to be would.

How nice that he'd finally come to his senses and realized that.

"Gosh, Santa," she said softly as she pulled the door open completely and stepped through it, "aren't you a little early this year? Christmas is still a week away."

"Ho, ho, hold that thought," he said with a smile. "You've been such a good girl this year, Santa just couldn't wait to get here."

She chuckled as the most wonderful tidings of comfort and joy began to unfold inside her. "Gee, I don't know, Santa," she objected halfheartedly. "I've been pretty cranky lately."

"Well, that happens to the best of us," he said. "Especially during the ho, ho, holidays."

She shook her head softly. "I don't think it's the holidays that's made me cranky, Santa. I love Christmas."

He nodded his understanding. "Well, it's tough to stay cheerful when you have to look for a new ho, ho, home, too."

She eyed him thoughtfully. "It's not the search for a new apartment, either. That particular problem has kind of been settled for me."

He smiled, a secret little smile that Mindy understood all too well. And at the knowledge of his feelings, her heart began to hammer hard in her chest.

"Well," Santa Reed began again, "I understand that morning sickness that comes with pregnancy can make you feel pretty ho, ho, horrible."

She waved a hand airily in front of herself. "Oh, that's been gone for months now."

"So, ho, ho…what's the problem then?"

She grinned slyly. "I think it must be all those licentious thoughts I've been having about a certain doctor for the past couple of weeks."

He held up a hand, palm out, clearly unconcerned. "Not a problem, as far as Santa is concerned." He lowered his voice and winked conspiratorially as he added, "Santa is only human, too, ya know. Like everyone else, he gets pretty ho-ho-horn—"

"I get the picture, Santa," Mindy cut him off with a laugh before he offended the real St. Nick. Then, before he had a chance to expound on the libido of a certain North Pole-dwelling denizen, she asked, "So…what's in the sack? Did you bring me a present?"

He wiggled his eyebrows playfully. "You bet. Like I said, you've been a *very* good girl this year. Come on in."

Only then did Mindy realize she still stood framed by the bedroom door, in the little hallway-alcove that led to the living room. Moving forward a few steps brought her completely into the room, and what she saw there took her breath away.

She had decorated the apartment a little bit, to satisfy her longing for Christmas trappings, had hung her paper chains and set her little tree on the counter linking the kitchen and living room. And she hadn't been able to resist buying a few more items, some peppermint-scented candles, which she'd placed on the coffee table, and a holly wreath with berries that she'd hung over the mantel of the gas fireplace.

But Reed had gone a few steps further. Not only had he lit her candles, but he'd added to them, a good dozen at least. Now all of them flickered happily to soften the darkness. A little tree, about three feet tall, sat on a table by the balcony doors, and several gifts of varying sizes, wrapped gaily in foil, lay beneath it. It was already decorated with tinsel and tiny ornaments, and multicolored lights that flashed off and on in an irregular rhythm. He must have done that part earlier, she thought, then plugged the thing in once he arrived. She marveled at his foresight and wondered just how long he'd been planning this whole thing.

"I came to my senses this afternoon," he said, seeming to read her mind in that maddening way he had.

Hope swelled within Mindy, but she'd been disappointed often enough in the past that she knew better than to let it get too far ahead of her. "What do you mean?" she asked.

He opened his mouth to respond, then seemed to remember something. "Hang on," he said. "I have to finish emptying my sack. Santa's work is never done, you know," he added parenthetically.

Mindy watched as he hastily completed his activities, and by the time he was finished, a veritable mountain of gifts had joined those wrapped presents beneath the tree. True to his tradition, Santa had brought a ton of toys, each and every one of them suited to a newborn, including, but not limited to, a colorful mobile for a crib, a brightly sewn quilt, an activity table full of moving, jangling objects, and—evidently, he hadn't been able to help himself—a tiny plush baseball and tiny plush bat to go with.

It was to those items that Mindy went first. "Aren't you presuming a little?" she asked. "What if it's a girl?"

"What if it is?" he asked from behind her. "She might just be one hell of a slugger."

Mindy laughed softly as she stood and took in the rest of

the loot. Tiny sweaters and booties and sleepers, little rattles and teethers and teddies. He must have spent hours shopping. No wonder he got home so late.

"I had help," he said, reading her mind again. "I told the salesclerk at the baby store that I was becoming a father in April and that I wanted to do something special for the mother of my child this Christmas."

Mindy spun around at his words, incredulous, sure she had misunderstood. But Reed only smiled at her.

"Before I left, the salesclerk told me my wife was one lucky woman to have me. I was going to disagree, but…" He lifted one shoulder and let it drop, but instead of looking careless, the gesture came off as anxious. "I thought maybe you should be the one to decide that," he said.

"What?" she asked. "Whether I'm lucky?"

He shook his head. "Whether you'll be my wife."

Her entire body went soft and lax at his remark. Tears filled her eyes, warmth filled her soul, love filled her heart. But all she could manage to say was, "Oh, Reed."

"So…what do you say?" he asked, his voice laced with an unmistakable uncertainty. "Will you marry me?"

He actually thought she might turn him down, Mindy realized. Then again, before she answered she had to know what his reasons really were. "Why do you want to marry me?" she asked him, point-blank.

His expression changed, becoming puzzled. "Isn't that obvious? Why do you think I want to marry you?"

"I don't know," she replied honestly. "Maybe because you want to take care of me? Because you don't think I can make it on my own? Because you feel obligated to me? Responsible for me?"

He nodded. "Yes to all of the above."

Her heart sank.

"Just like I want *you* to take care of *me*. And because I don't think I can make it on my own. And because I hope *you* feel obligated to me, responsible for *me*." He took a few steps forward, then stopped, still obviously not sure of his reception.

"Mostly, though, Mindy, I want to marry you because I love you. Because these last two weeks, I've felt more alive, more human, more wonderful, than I've ever felt in my entire life. And because I can't imagine my life without you. It would be so empty. So lonely. So awful. I love you, Mindy," he said again, a little more desperately. "I love you so much."

She could see by the look in his eyes that he was telling her the truth, and the hope that she'd let simmer inside her bubbled up unrestrained as a result. Unable to help herself, she hurtled herself at him, threw her arms around his neck and kissed him for all she was worth.

Reed took Mindy's action to be a very good sign. Still, he'd never been one to get overly optimistic, so he pulled back from her long enough to gaze down into her face. "Is that a yes?" he asked.

She nodded. "That's a 'You bet your life I'll marry you.' Oh, I love you so much."

He would have settled for a simple yes, but, hey, why worry about particulars? "In that case," he said, releasing her long enough to reach into the pocket of his big Santa pants, "I think you should open this present first."

He extended a cube-shaped, palm-sized box covered with dove gray velvet. Mindy smiled shyly as she took it from him, her green eyes seeming deeper somehow, more expressive. Her cheeks were pink with her heightened emotion, and he felt just so damned grateful that she would want him. When she opened the box, she gasped at the ring within, and he thought that, too, was a very good sign.

"It's beautiful," she said of the one-carat, heart-shaped solitaire, her voice a scant whisper.

"You think?" he asked, relief filling him. "I wasn't sure you'd like it."

"I love it," she said. "I love you for choosing it. It's just so…"

"It reminded me of you for some reason," he told her when her voice trailed off. "Maybe because it's so brilliant and beautiful. Or maybe because it made me smile."

It made her smile, too, he noted. "Put it on me," she said without preamble. "I want to see how it looks."

He immediately obeyed her request, sliding the ring easily over the fourth finger of her left hand. She held it up to the twinkling Christmas lights to admire it, and Reed watched as the flicker and flash of color wreaked havoc with the stone.

"You know," he said, "to get the full effect of that, you should probably be naked."

She laughed. "Gosh, how do you always manage to read my mind?"

"Guess we're just two of a kind," he told her.

"Guess we are," she agreed.

He moved behind her, telling himself he wanted to have the same view of the ring that she had, but deep down, he knew it was really just because he wanted to unbutton her pajama shirt. She didn't object as he lifted his fingers to the first button, only continued to gaze at her new ring with *much* affection. So he pushed the button through its hole, looking over her shoulder to see where the next one lay. When he did, he noted the way the soft flannel parted to give him just a shadowed hint of the creamy flesh beneath.

And suddenly, it seemed essential that they *both* be naked to receive the full benefit of her ring. So, with a few more swift maneuvers, he freed the remaining buttons on her shirt. But still, Mindy seemed not to notice his actions, because she was so focused on the ring. So Reed curled his fingers into the collar of her shirt and pulled it off her, tossing it into a neglected pile on the floor.

"Wow, that helped a lot," she said, still staring at the ring. "Without the distraction of my pajama top, this puppy really sparkles."

"Amazing," Reed said, even though he wasn't looking at her ring. Instead, he had trained his attention on the twin globes of her breasts that beckoned him. Without hesitation, he filled each hand with one, rolling her erect nipples between his thumbs and forefingers. That, finally, seemed to get

Mindy's attention, because she reached both hands back to curl her fingers into his hair.

And, very softly, very wantonly, she said, "Oh, Reed. Do that again."

She didn't have to ask him twice. He nuzzled the soft juncture of her neck and shoulder, brushing soft, butterfly kisses along the elegant curve. Then he moved one hand lower, to her gently rounded belly, splaying his fingers open before pushing her back against him. Her fanny settled against that hard, heated part of him, and he grew more rigid. She must have sensed that too, because she instinctively pushed her bottom more intimately against him and tightened her fingers in his hair.

He loved the way her body felt, so lush, round and ripe. And he made a mental note to put another baby inside her someday so that he could enjoy this vision of her again. Until that day came, however, he was perfectly content with the situation as it was. He and Mindy were going to have a baby. And they were going to be married. And they would be in love forever.

A family, that's what Reed was getting for Christmas. And he couldn't be more pleased.

That idea alone hardened him more, and he moved the hand on her belly lower, to the drawstring of her pajama bottoms. With one deft gesture, he loosed it, then settled both hands at her hips to push the fabric down. When the soft flannel pooled around her ankles, Mindy stepped out of it, but she made no move to turn around. Feeling more erotic by the moment, Reed took advantage of her position to explore every inch of her front, loving all the wispy, wanton little sounds she made whenever he discovered a new place. Eventually, though, his hand gravitated toward that heated, feminine core between her legs, and Mindy's reaction grew more fervent.

She spread her legs when she noted his intention, allowing him fuller access, and he buried his fingers in the soft, damp folds he found there. Over and over, he pillaged her, plundered her, penetrated her, until her breathing came in ragged, hiccuping little gasps. With his other hand, he freed the oversize buckle on his Santa suit, grateful for the first time for how big the damned thing was. The pants fell easily to the ground, and with some quick maneuvering, his briefs and too-big boots followed. The coat went next, and then he and Mindy were both pressed against each other, back to front, spoon-fashion, naked.

Unable to wait any longer, Reed entered her that way, and Mindy uttered a delicious sound of contentment and need as she bent forward a bit. Gripping her hips, he withdrew some, then dove deep again, feeling not as if he were filling her, but as if she were filling him instead. And with every stroke, he wanted more, so more was what he took. For a long time, they coupled that way, until Reed felt himself letting go inside.

He withdrew completely then and turned her around to face him, urging both their bodies to the ground. And there, beside the Christmas tree, he knelt before her, then lowered her down to his lap. She knelt astride him, facing him, on top of him. And this time when Reed entered her, he did it slowly, completely, eternally. Very gradually, Mindy inched her body up, then down, taking more of him inside her with every movement. She wrapped her arms around his neck and covered his mouth with hers, and he filled his hands with her breast and bottom, and kissed her to the depths of his soul.

When they climaxed, it was as one, each of them crying out their utter astonishment that two souls could meld so perfectly, so completely, so beautifully.

So timelessly.

And a long time later, as they lay side by side in the big bed, clinging to each other, they were no less dazed and happy. Reed pulled Mindy against him, her back to his front, as it had all begun earlier, and spread both of his hands open over her belly. Beneath his fingertips, he thought he felt a faint fluttering of life, and he smiled. Surely it was far too soon for him to be feeling such a thing. But wasn't it incredible that there was indeed life in there to feel?

And better still, that there was life out here to live?

''Merry Christmas, Mindy,'' he said tenderly again as he stroked his hands over her soft, taut flesh.

She curled her fingers over his hands and pressed hard. ''Merry Christmas, Reed.'' And then, very softly, she added, ''As I was lying here in bed earlier tonight, I was so afraid you weren't going to come home.''

He said nothing for a moment, then, very softly, told her, ''Yeah, so was I. And for a lot longer than just tonight. Fortunately, this year, for the first time in my life, I got exactly what I wanted for Christmas.''

She snuggled closer to him and said in a tired, sleepy voice, ''Yeah, me, too.''

* * * * *

Don't miss Elizabeth Bevarly's next book in the FROM HERE TO MATERNITY *mini-series,* Dr Mummy, *available in February 2001, only from Desire™!*

Silhouette Stars

Born this Month

Monica Seles, Walt Disney, Jeff Bridges, James Galway, Frank Sinatra, Lee Remick, Keith Richards, Jenny Agutter, Uri Geller, Mary Tyler Moore

Star of the Month

Sagittarius

A year of progress in many areas of your life, however, effort will be needed to organise yourself properly in order to make the best of what is on offer. Romance is well aspected and you could find yourself making a commitment early next year. Take care over finances, read all the small print before signing contracts.

SILH/HR/0012a

 **Capricorn**

A career move is on the cards but you will need to decide if it is what you want. It could be worth all the disruption that it might cause to your life.

Aquarius

A happy go lucky month with lots of social events on offer. Forget your troubles and catch up on old friends and with opportunities to make new ones too, you should have a ball!

 Pisces

There is the promise of a brighter, happier period in which you may achieve something that's been top of your wish-list for a long while. You could surprise a lot of people, not least yourself!

Aries

The focus is on the home where you will find real happiness and contentment. Old friends make contact and you may be planning an 'out of the ordinary' holiday together.

 Taurus

A busy month with plenty to be done around the home. Enlist the help of those around to make the job quicker and allow you time to relax as well. A touching surprise from a loved one could really lift your spirits.

Gemini

There should be good reason to celebrate this month as the dark clouds lift and you see your life progressing positively. One particular gift brings a wry smile to your face.

Cancer

Listen to your inner soul and act on what you really feel as it could save you from making a big mistake. An old friend re-enters your life late in the month.

Leo

A new opportunity to study, re-train or work in an area that suits you should not be missed. A loved one could pleasantly surprise you mid-month.

 Virgo

A great time to start a new project as you should be feeling very creative. A romantic encounter sets your pulse racing, but take care, all may not be as it seems.

Libra

Wipe away the winter blues, take up a new activity, revamp the home. By keeping busy you will feel more positive and your energy will create opportunity.

 Scorpio

You should be in a position to make the most of the golden opportunities on offer. Those around you will be happy to support you during this exciting period, so go for it!

Look out for more
Silhouette Stars next month

SILHOUETTE
DESIRE®

AVAILABLE FROM 22ND DECEMBER 2000

A BRIDE FOR JACKSON POWERS Dixie Browning

Man of the Month

Jackson Powers has only recently discovered he has a baby daughter and sultry stranger Hetty Reynolds is willing to help him find the road to fatherhood. *And* the road to wedded bliss...

THE PRINCESS'S WHITE KNIGHT Carla Cassidy

Royally Wed

A regal princess let loose in the world needed more than a bodyguard—she needed a husband. So royal protector Gabriel Morgan married Princess Serena Wyndham in-name-only. Could this marriage-of-convenience result in a happy-ever-after?

THE DOCTOR WORE SPURS Leanne Banks

Handsome bachelor Dr Tyler Logan always got what he wanted, but when he went to Jill Hershey for fundraising advice he got a lot more than he expected!

MERCENARY'S WOMAN Diana Palmer

Soldiers of Fortune

Sweet Sally Johnson was in danger and Ebenezer Scott fought to protect her. But she yearned for so much more. Could she slip through his defences and become this beloved mercenary's bride?

DID YOU SAY MARRIED?! Kathie DeNosky

Opposites Chance Warren and Kristen Lassiter not only wake up together after a very steamy night, but then find they are married— Vegas-style! Thrown into wedlock, the pair prepare for a baby-on-the-way...

GOING...GOING...WED! Amy J. Fetzer

The Bridal Bid

Bought at a charity auction, Madison Holt was meant to provide domestic help to businessman Alex Donahue. But her innocent kisses had this marriage-shy millionaire dreaming about a different kind of arrangement...

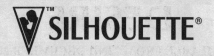

FREE
2 BOOKS
AND A SURPRISE GIFT!

We would like to take this opportunity to thank you for reading this Silhouette® book by offering you the chance to take TWO more specially selected titles from the Desire™ series absolutely FREE! We're also making this offer to introduce you to the benefits of the Reader Service™—

- ★ FREE home delivery
- ★ FREE monthly Newsletter
- ★ FREE gifts and competitions
- ★ Exclusive Reader Service discounts
- ★ Books available before they're in the shops

Accepting these FREE books and gift places you under no obligation to buy; you may cancel at any time, even after receiving your free shipment. Simply complete your details below and return the entire page to the address below. *You don't even need a stamp!*

YES! Please send me 2 free Desire books and a surprise gift. I understand that unless you hear from me, I will receive 4 superb new titles every month for just £2.70 each, postage and packing free. I am under no obligation to purchase any books and may cancel my subscription at any time. The free books and gift will be mine to keep in any case.

D0ZEC

Ms/Mrs/Miss/Mr ....Initials...
BLOCK CAPITALS PLEASE

Surname...

Address...

....

....Postcode ....

Send this whole page to:
UK: FREEPOST CN81, Croydon, CR9 3WZ
EIRE: PO Box 4546, Kilcock, County Kildare (stamp required)